She'd slept with the enemy

All of a sudden the full impact of what Liana had allowed to happen struck her. "I think you'd better leave," she said in a low voice.

Max's mouth tightened, but then he nodded curtly. "You're too scared of your own feelings to see reason right now. I'll call you later."

"Don't bother. I don't think it's a good idea for us to be, uh... seeing each other."

He crossed the room and stopped in front of her. "You can't mean that. Not after the way you gave yourself to me last night."

Liana steeled herself against the sensual memories. "I wasn't thinking clearly. I am now."

Max slid his fingers through her hair and pulled her close. His warm mouth closed over hers and he kissed her until she was gasping and trembling. Then he drew back and looked directly into her eyes. "You're the best thing that's happened to me in a long time. I'm not giving _____ a fight."

For James—again—with love
And for Wyn,
who always gives so generously of her time

———— ~ ————

Beguiled

DAWN CARROLL

MILLS & BOON LIMITED
ETON HOUSE, 18-24 PARADISE ROAD
RICHMOND, SURREY TW9 1SR

*First published in Great Britain in 1993
by Mills & Boon Limited, Eton House, 18-24 Paradise Road,
Richmond, Surrey TW9 1SR*

© Dawn Carol Boese 1992

ISBN 0 263 78385 5

21 - 9308

Made and printed in Great Britain

1

SO, THE RUMORS WERE true. "Bambi-eyes" was back.
Max Valentin's grip tightened reflexively on the binoculars he held. For a moment he lost sight of the
woman he'd been watching from the balcony of his
small white stucco house. Exhaling an impatient sound,
he leaned against the black wrought-iron railing and
used the powerful lenses of the binoculars to sweep the
area where he'd last seen her. At first, he saw only
gently rolling hills, swathed with vapor turned irides-
cent by the first rays of sunshine. As always, the sight
filled him with awe. The valley's ancient Native American settlers must have been similarly affected because
they had named it Temecula, meaning "sunlight on the
mist." Almost every day, he took a few minutes to enjoy the peaceful landscape including the acres of vineyards that surrounded his home.

He spotted the woman again, a tall slender figure
dressed in shorts and T-shirt, poised at the edge of an
oak-shaded pond. A brightly colored towel was draped
casually over one shoulder. He adjusted the focus for a
closer look, captivated by the way her long raven-black
hair glinted in the brightening rays of the sun. Her skin
was the color of orange-blossom honey. If it hadn't been
for her modern clothing, she would have passed for an

American Indian maiden from Temecula's bygone days, preparing for her morning bath.

"Liana," he murmured, feeling a sudden constriction in his chest. Liana Castillo. Lord, what memories that name evoked.

She stretched, then, arching her body toward the warmth of the sun, and his breath caught. Gone was the boyish fourteen-year-old's figure he remembered. Lush womanly curves strained the thin fabric of her T-shirt and denim shorts. He felt a shaft of desire flash through him as he stared, transfixed. Fourteen years had made a hell of a difference in Frank Castillo's daughter. Although, she'd always been a captivating little waif, with those big, doe-soft eyes of hers. Bambi eyes. Their startling greenish-brown color could ensnare a man in an instant. And then there'd been her full, slightly pouting mouth....

Max yanked himself out of the past and grunted in annoyance. He'd learned once how seductive Liana Castillo could be, and according to timeworn gossip, he wasn't the only one. Not that he put much store in gossip. He'd borne the brunt of its gross inaccuracies too many times. But he did know that both Liana and her older sister, Serena, had been key figures in a tragedy that had once rocked the quiet community of Temecula.

"Enjoying the view?"

Max started guiltily at the sound that came from behind him, but his guilt quickly turned to irritation as he lowered the glasses and swung around to face his stepmother. Framed in the doorway leading from the upper hallway, Sybille Valentin regarded him with shrewd brown eyes. A striking woman of fifty years, she looked much younger due to her own tireless efforts and the skill of a plastic surgeon. Her light brown hair was stylishly cut, and she dressed with the casual elegance Frenchwomen seemed to come by naturally. Many people considered her beautiful, but Max had never been able to see beyond her manipulative personality.

She couldn't possibly have known what he was looking at, he assured himself firmly. Without the aid of binoculars, the pond was just a faint silver flash in a distant stand of trees. Aside from that, at thirty-three, he didn't owe her any explanations. They'd settled that issue years ago after his father's death, when Max had returned home from France to assume control of Valentin's Winery.

He ignored her question and said, "Weather looks good—visiting will probably be heavier today." Sybille was in charge of the tours and tasting room at the winery—an arrangement that allowed her to feel useful, without forcing him to have too much contact with her. He still retained a residue of resentment for the unhappiness she'd brought to his father and himself. His father had met and married her during a visit to France, where he'd gone to escape his grief over his first wife's death. Fifteen years his junior, Sybille had offered him a smoldering sensuality that he'd believed could take the place of real love. After they'd returned to America with her troublesome ten-year-old son, Rennie, even Max had been able to see it wasn't a love match. When the fires of passion had burned out, all that remained were discontent and resentment. Their arguments, made frighteningly intense by Sybille's fiery temper, had often driven Max from the house.

Now, his relationship with his stepmother was based on tolerance, rather than filial devotion. He chose to live in the small house that had once belonged to his grandparents, rather than share the larger main house, which stood a short distance away. The arrangement prevented a lot of problems, especially since Sybille had developed a suspiciously avid interest in the young man who did odd jobs for her.

He turned to regard the acres of grapevines lined up like leafy sentinels along the property. The vineyard and the prizewinning wines he created were the only things that really mattered to him now. In recent years, Temecula Valley wines had been garnering national attention, and more than anything, he wanted to grab a piece of that market. Only one obstacle stood in the way of expansion—the lease that Frank Castillo held on the adjoining land.

"Speaking of visitors," Sybille went on, her voice deepening with innuendo, "I was right about Liana Castillo. She arrived yesterday, and already that crazy father of hers is raving to everyone about how she's going to save his run-down horse ranch. He's probably even told her that nonsense about someone trying to kill him."

Max shrugged. "I doubt she'll believe that. The sheriff's department hasn't."

Sybille came over to stand beside him, her expression suddenly intense. "She might. I always thought she and that older sister of hers were a little off. After the accident, she definitely wasn't right in the head."

Max gritted his teeth. He was sick to death of hearing about the accident. He hadn't even been in the country twelve years ago, but he knew every detail of the car wreck that had claimed the lives of his stepbrother Rennie, Liana's older sister, Serena, and Rennie's friend, Arlie Moser. Liana had emerged from the twisted wreckage virtually unharmed, although rumor had it that she'd lost her ability to speak as a result of the experience. He'd also heard Sybille bemoan the fact that she'd been left to face the scandal surrounding her poor Rennie's death, while Liana had run off to live with relatives in Oregon.

Poor Rennie. Max's mouth tightened. Rennie had been a poor excuse for a human being. Even in his death he'd shamed his adoptive family. He'd been drinking heavily the night of the accident, which was why he'd lost control of the car. Not long after, word had gotten out that Serena had been pregnant with his illegitimate child the night she died.

Beside him, Sybille made an impatient sound. "I can see there's no point in discussing this with you."

He glanced at her in surprise. "What is there to discuss?"

Sybille gestured in the general direction of the neighboring property. "The lease you hold on Castillo's land, of course. If he goes through with his threats to exercise his option to buy, we won't be able to expand next year. But now that his daughter's here, there might be a chance that you can talk her into changing the stubborn old fool's mind." Sybille smirked a little. "After all, you obviously know how to handle women. Half of the female population in the valley would do anything you asked."

Max shot her a warning glare. He hated references to his reputation as a local Lothario, even if there had been a time when he deserved it. "There's a good possibility Liana's come back to help her father defeat my plans, especially if she hates the Valentin family as much as he does."

Sybille humphed, her expression self-righteous. "I learned to forgive and forget. Why can't they? After all, my loss was as great as theirs. Maybe greater. Rennie *was* my only son." She shook her head sorrowfully. "Hanging on to hatred is like taking poison. If you ask me, *that* is what's killing Frank Castillo."

Max grunted noncommittally and refrained from pointing out that Sybille certainly hadn't forgotten the Castillo's involvement in the accident.

"Still," she continued, undaunted by his unencouraging response, "the girl *has* been away for a long time. Perhaps she doesn't share the old man's grudge. You could at least try talking to her, no?"

Max eyed her for a moment, then turned and started inside without deigning to answer. He fully intended to talk to Liana Castillo. That had been decided the moment he spotted her with the binoculars.

"Max!" The sharp edge of resentment in Sybille's voice made him pause and look back. "I'm only trying to help you regain what is rightfully yours," she said, her dark eyes burning with unexpected vehemence.

Yes, mine, he thought. His father had left everything to him, except for an endowment that allotted Sybille a portion of the winery's profits each year until she remarried. She had no say in the running of the place, but his father had made a dying request that she be allowed to live and continue working there for as long as she wished. Even though her personality rubbed Max the wrong way, he had to admit she worked hard. They managed to avoid open warfare, as long as she didn't try to tell him how to run his business. "I appreciate your concern," he replied with quiet authority. "But I'm capable of handling the situation without your help."

Sybille's head jerked back as if from a blow, but then she nodded, visibly bringing her vexation under control. "Of course, Max," she said a bit stiffly. "I've never thought otherwise."

"Good." He paused, then added, "Next time you drop by, please knock before entering."

GASPING, LIANA SURFACED from the pond's chilly water. Despite the lack of warmth, she felt better. The bracing effect offered a respite from the deepening gloom she'd been feeling since she'd arrived yesterday.

So many changes, she thought, sweeping away the drops of water clinging to her lashes. The sleepy little valley of Temecula had become a bedroom community for the city-weary Yuppies from San Diego and Los Angeles. Once there had been a small town with an unpaved main street and a dusty collection of ancient buildings. Now traffic jammed the four-lane paved street, which was lined with an overwhelming array of shops, businesses and fast-food restaurants. In place of vast stretches of open land, there were modern, up-scale housing developments.

Worst of all was the change at home. Castillo's Arabians had once been a first-rate breeding and boarding ranch, its boundaries marked off by pristine white fences, its reputation impeccable. Now it lay in a shocking state of disrepair, the stable nearly empty, the board fences weathered gray and bare of paint. Even more shocking, her dad looked just as weathered and gray as the wood.

She closed her eyes. When had she seen him last? Two years ago? Yes, that was it, at John's funeral. He hadn't looked so old and frail then—had he? Or had she been too wrapped up in her own grief to see it? She winced and pressed her fingers against the sudden tension between her eyebrows. Perhaps she hadn't wanted to face the possibility of coming back here. Yet she hadn't hesitated when he had called last week, claiming that the Valentin family was trying to take his land away from him. He'd even hinted about attempts on his life. Hearing that, she'd thought her father was being a bit paranoid. But she didn't have any trouble believing that Max Valentin might want to repossess her father's land. She'd learned long ago how heartless Valentin men could be.

A twig snapped nearby and she quickly turned toward the sound. A tall masculine figure appeared from among the oak trees at the pond's shore. Every nerve-ending within her went taut with recognition. Maximilian Valentin. She would have known that devastatingly handsome face anywhere. It was the face of the man who'd once stolen her heart and then callously tossed it aside.

"Liana." The deep resonant bass sent a shock wave through her. The tone of his voice had matured from the uncertain baritone of youth to a richer, more commanding timbre. It was a man's voice, and it fit perfectly with the solidly muscled physique that filled out his chambray shirt and jeans. There were subtle changes in his face, too. Deep creases bracketed the firm, wide mouth, and although his lower lip still had a sensual curve to it, she thought she detected a twist of cynicism that hadn't been there before. The densely-lashed eyes still reminded her of sapphires, but they no longer held the guileless charm of callow youth. Now, those blue depths conveyed experience—and promised sensual delight. The only thing that hadn't changed was his thick, slightly wavy hair, as black as her own.

"Liana," he repeated, making her realize she'd been staring at him in silence. "I'd heard that you were back."

She opened her mouth to respond, but her vocal chords refused to cooperate. Frowning, she swallowed against the constriction, a stress-related vestige of the hysterical mutism she'd overcome long ago.

His expression reflected instant alarm, and when he spoke again he did so louder, as many people instinctively did when dealing with the deaf. "They said you'd lost your voice, but I thought . . ." He gestured helplessly. "I don't know sign language. . . ."

She shook her head, and opened her mouth to speak, then on impulse held back, just to see what he'd do. She wasn't the lovesick girl he'd rejected so long ago. Nor was she the emotionally devastated teenager who'd run away from her problems. She'd worked long and hard to become a strong, self-possessed woman who knew how to stand firm when necessary. But Max didn't know that. It might work to her advantage to keep him in the dark for a while, if he really was after her father's land.

Max cleared his throat. "You've certainly grown up," he said, his gaze flickering downward from her face just long enough to remind her of the thin wet T-shirt that clung to her skin. Even from a distance of at least ten yards she could see the appreciation in his eyes. She crossed her arms over her breasts and quickly sank down into the water until it touched her chin. His blatant gaze didn't surprise her. According to her father, Max wasn't a likely candidate for a monastery. In his teen years, he'd been known as a real heartbreaker, with a reputation he'd reportedly worked hard to maintain when he went off to study viticulture at UC, Davis. From there he'd gone to France to serve an apprenticeship with relatives in the wine industry, and she could just imagine the effect he'd had on females in that country.

Not that she cared, she told herself quickly. The whole idea of passion left her cold—as cold as the water surrounding her. Yet, as Max began to walk toward her along the edge of the pond, an unexpected heat seemed to surge through her chilled body, as if a fire long banked had suddenly sprung to life.

Unnerved, she forgot her resolution to keep silent. "Are you in the habit of trespassing on my father's property?" she inquired sarcastically.

Max looked startled for a moment, then gave her an accusing frown. "So, you can speak. Why didn't you say something sooner?"

She frowned back at him. "I didn't have anything to say to you. Now, would you please leave? I'd like to get out of the water."

He came to stand at the water's edge and folded his arms across his chest. "Go ahead. I won't stand in your way. And I'm not trespassing. I hold the lease on this land, remember? That makes it legally mine."

Noting the firm set of his jaw, she began to realize that her father had been right. Max fully intended to reclaim his land. He just might succeed, considering her father's current financial state.

"The property won't be yours when my father exercises his option to buy three months from now," she shot back. "Now, will you go?"

He shook his head and smiled unexpectedly. "Well, well, little Liana has grown some spunk. Does that mean you intend to help your father in his crazy plan to keep that run-down ranch?"

"I might, if it means keeping it away from you. And I'm not "little Liana" anymore. I've done a lot of growing since the last time you saw me."

Max's smile widened. "I believe I already commented on that. Now, why don't you come out of that water so we can discuss this like adults? Your lips are turning blue." He bent to scoop up the large yellow towel she'd left draped over a nearby bush. "Come on. I promise not to look, if that's what you're afraid of." He held the towel out invitingly.

"I'm n-not a-afraid of you," she said, her teeth beginning to chatter. "I just have a n-normal sense of m-modesty, if you don't m-mind."

"Fine, my eyes are shut." He made a great show of squeezing his eyes closed.

Liana considered her options and decided she'd better get out of the water. Max didn't look as if he'd move an inch until she turned blue all over. Her teeth set—partly in frustration, partly to keep them from clacking together like castanets—she waded out of the pond. In her haste to grab the towel from him, she forgot to look where she was stepping, and in the next instant she felt a sharp pain on the sole of her foot. Gasping, she hopped back on her uninjured foot and would have toppled to the pebble-strewn bank if the towel and a pair of strong arms hadn't suddenly been wrapped around her. Her feet lost contact with the ground as he swept her up and seated her on a grassy area by the pond.

"What are you doing?" she demanded, as he crouched down beside her and captured the ankle of her hurt foot with one large hand.

"Rescuing you, I thought. Is this the foot you hurt?"

"It's nothing," she said, trying to jerk away, to no avail.

"Hold still, damn it. I want to see if you have a puncture wound."

She increased her efforts to twist out of his ironlike grip. "There's no need. I'll take care of it myself. In fact, my ankle hurts more than the sole of my foot, at the moment. Will you please let go?"

He didn't let go, but his grasp loosened a little. "It wouldn't hurt if you'd stop struggling." He gave her a significant look, letting his gaze drop to her chest. "You'd be better off concentrating on keeping that towel around you."

She glanced down and realized she'd allowed the towel to drop away. Her only covering at the moment was the wet T-shirt, which clung with embarrassing faithfulness to her breasts. Through the damp fabric the dark rose outline of her nipples could be seen clearly. With a sharp exclamation, she snatched up the towel and clasped it in front of her.

As she did so, Max gave her foot a thorough check. "No puncture. That's good." Then he surprised her by running his forefinger lightly over the highly sensitive sole, making her jerk back again. This time he released her with a grin. "You weren't such a tenderfoot when you were a kid. You used to run around barefoot all summer."

She wrapped the towel more firmly around herself and glared at him. Hearing him refer to the past gave her an odd feeling, as if an old locked door had begun to creak open. "A lot of things have changed since then."

His voice lowered with innuendo. "I'll say."

Uttering a soft growl of outrage, she retorted, "A gentleman wouldn't have said that. But then, you never were much of a gentleman, were you, Max? You were more the love-'em-and-leave-'em type."

His eyebrows rose slightly, then lowered in a frown, telling her she'd scored a hit. "That may have been true once," he admitted irritably. "But I've changed, too."

"Not according to what I've heard."

He rose suddenly to tower over her, his six-foot frame rather daunting. "Before you believe everything you hear from the local gossips, keep in mind that they had quite a bit to say about you a while ago."

Like the repercussion of a distant explosion, the old hurt accosted her, not as painfully as it had originally, but it was inescapable, nonetheless. Even after the passage of years she could still see the censuring eyes and hear the whispered comments, some of them actually suggesting that she and her sister had gotten what they deserved. "I suppose you believed them, too," she said bitterly.

Max folded his arms over his chest. "I wasn't here when it happened, so I'm not sure what to believe. I do know that Rennie was a hellion. He brought nothing but grief to my family from the day my father married his mother. But I don't know if anyone with Bambi eyes should be trusted. I remember how it felt when you used them on me."

Liana tensed, remembering the time she'd developed a foolish crush on Max Valentin. At the age of twelve, she'd been painfully shy and uncomfortable with boys her own age. Five years her senior, Max had seemed like the epitome of manhood in her inexperienced eyes.

For two years she'd secretly cherished her love for him. Then, the one time she found the courage to let her feelings show, the result had been so devastating she'd vowed never to risk that kind of hurt again. She hadn't even dated anyone up until the fateful night of the accident. Even then, she had only gone out with Arlie because of Rennie's endless taunting.

Agitated by the memory, she jumped up to face him, still clutching the towel. Even though she considered herself above average height at five feet eight inches, she had to look up to meet his eyes. "What I remember," she snapped, "are all the reasons I have for not liking you, Max Valentin. You're no better than those gossips who judged me and my sister without bothering to look for the truth."

For a moment, Max seemed taken aback. Then a smile tugged at the corners of his mouth. "There's that spunk again. I can hardly believe it. You were such a timid little thing as a kid."

There had been a time, once, when his smile had thrilled her to the soles of her feet. Now it only irritated her further. "You're going to see a lot more of my 'spunk,' if you have any ideas about trying to take over my father's land."

Max cocked an eyebrow at her. "So, you really think you can help him? Too bad. I'd hoped you might be willing to listen to reason. It'll take a minor miracle to get that ranch back on its feet."

The confidence with which he spoke made Liana shiver with unease, but she hid it behind a confident smile. Even though she had a suspicion it might take more than a miracle to restore Castillo's Arabians, she'd never admit it to him. "I've been known to perform a few financial miracles in the past," she said, and was gratified to see a shadow of uncertainty cross his face.

"How do you intend to go about it?"

"Stick around and watch," she replied archly. Buoyed by the feeling of having gained the upper hand—at least temporarily—she turned and stalked away, her head held high.

MAX WATCHED HER GO with a strange mixture of emotions, not the least of which was a grudging admiration. Sometime during the years since he'd last seen her, Liana Castillo had developed a backbone, and he found it damned attractive, even if it did mean fighting her for what he wanted. He grimaced. Actually, her backbone wasn't the only part of her that he found attractive....

He inhaled slowly, closing his eyes to recall the breathtaking vision of her breasts straining against the clinging, transparent fabric of her T-shirt. She'd been lovely as a child, but womanhood had turned her into a stunning beauty. From the moment she'd stood up to him, he'd felt a resurgence of the powerful feelings she'd stirred in him so long ago. The five-year age difference that had been prohibitive when they were younger, no longer seemed significant. Of course, there was the little problem of her dislike for him....

Lost in his thoughts, Max started back the way he'd come and nearly tripped over a pair of white sandals lying in his path. He stooped to pick them up. *Well, Liana, it looks like I have a good excuse to see you again.* Smiling, he headed for home, the sandals dangling from one long, work-toughened finger.

LIANA'S BRAVADO CARRIED her halfway back to her father's house before she realized she'd forgotten her sandals. She hesitated, muttering to herself, then decided that sore feet were preferable to going back to the pond and risking another confrontation with Max Valentin. Actually, the dusty path, which led through the back pasture, wasn't that hard on her feet.

What *did* hurt was looking around at the empty weed-infested enclosure that had once contained half a dozen or more sleek and healthy Arabian brood-mares. The faded red stable, the scattered outbuildings and the two-story white frame house—all were in desperate need of paint. Only the massive oak trees that shaded the house and lined the long driveway had remained the same.

Her father's sole income came from several quarter horses that he boarded for people who lived in one of Temecula's ritzy new housing developments. The only vestige of the once-thriving Castillo's Arabians was an ill-tempered stallion named Son of the Sheik, or Sonny. With the last of his savings, her father had purchased the animal several years ago in the hope that the stud fees he'd earn would provide the capital to rebuild the ranch. So far, that hadn't happened, but Frank Castillo's faith in the animal remained undaunted.

Personally, Liana had disliked the beast on sight. When her father had taken her out to the stable last night to show off his prize, Sonny had laid his ears back and tried to bite her. Not to say that he wasn't a beautiful-looking Arabian, she thought, scuffing her feet in the sun-warmed dirt as she walked.

The high-pitched whinny of a horse cut through the morning air, followed by a loud bang and a man's angry shout. Yanked out of her thoughts, Liana looked toward the stable and cried, "Dad!" She gripped the towel tightly around her and ran.

2

LIANA DASHED INSIDE the stable, then slowed to a walk while her eyes adjusted to the dim interior. "Dad?" she called anxiously. "Where are you?" Relief swept over her when she saw his shadowy figure step out of a stall at the end of the structure.

"I'm here, Liana. What's wrong?"

"I was about to ask you that," she said, moving toward him. A man of average height, Frank Castillo had always given the impression of great stature with his broad shoulders and proud bearing. Now his shoulders looked thin and stooped, and his once-jet-black hair had faded to pale silver. Even his eyes, formerly such a piercing brown, seemed cloudy and dim. Liana stopped in front of him, trying to hide her distress. "I heard Sonny carrying on, and thought—"

"It's nothing," her father interjected quickly. "He's just feeling his oats this morning." He glanced at the damp towel she wore. "Been to the pond, I see. Are you ready for some breakfast? I could fix you something as soon as I'm through here."

"I think I should take care of the cooking while I'm here. You have enough on your hands with the outside work." She glanced around and tried not to show her dismay. Her father must have been feeling ill for some

time to have let the place go like this. "Tell you what,
I'll fix breakfast while you finish whatever you were
doing, and then we can have a little talk while we eat.
I have a lot of questions."

Her father sighed and looked around the shabby
stable, obviously seeing it as she had. "I suppose you
do, honey. Looks pretty hopeless, doesn't it?"

For a moment he looked so old and beaten, her heart
nearly broke. "Not necessarily," she hedged, unwilling
to admit her true feelings. "I only wish you had called
me sooner."

"I wouldn't have called when I did, if it weren't for
Valentin and his plans to take my land." Liana didn't
think it would be a good idea to tell her father about the
encounter she'd just had with Max at the pond. His
feelings about the Valentins were strong enough as it
was. "Well, I'm here now. And I want to hear everything—over breakfast."

Her father nodded in resignation. "All right. I'll be
up to the house in about half an hour." As she hurried
out the big double doors, he called after her, "Be sure
to make the coffee extra strong."

FORTY MINUTES LATER, they faced each other over the
oilcloth-covered table in the large, dingy kitchen. Remembering how it used to look deepened Liana's mel-
ancholy. At one time the cupboards had been pristine
white, the linoleum floor immaculate, the gingham
curtains crisp and fresh. Even after her mother had
died, there had been a housekeeper who kept it look-

ing nice. Now the place cried out for a good cleaning. Liana added that chore to the growing list in her head.

"I'm sorry about the way the place looks," her father said for at least the hundredth time since her arrival yesterday. "I just can't move as fast as I used to. And I haven't been able to afford hired help for a while." He glanced down at the scrambled eggs and toast on his plate. "It's been some time since I had food this good." He offered her a teasing grin that reminded her of the warm laughing man he'd once been. "Never could stand my own cooking."

"Oh, Dad!" she exclaimed, fighting tears. "How could you have let things get this bad before contacting me? Did you think I'd refuse to help you?"

He reached over to pat her hand awkwardly. "No, honey. I was doing okay for quite a while after you went to live with your aunt Opal. About the time I started having real trouble, you married John. I sure as heck wasn't going to drag you away from your new husband." He sighed and squeezed her hand. "Then, when he died . . . Well, I figured you didn't need any more worries."

Liana shook her head, a certain sadness tugging at her heart, as it always did at the thought of her late husband. "But that was two years ago. I grieved for John, but you're important to me, too. Surely you could have—"

"No," he interrupted gently. "You seemed to be doing well in Oregon. I didn't want to take you away from that—not when I knew the horrible memories you had of this place."

Oh, Dad, you only knew half of them, she reflected.
After years of therapy she had learned to let the excruciating images of that night blur into an amorphous
mass, a distant pain like the ache of an amputated limb.
But certain aspects still haunted her—certain things she
would never overcome. The night of the accident, she'd
lost more than her sister: her innocence had been rav-
aged by a brutal act that had changed her forever.

Her father's gruff voice drew her back to the present.
"I can see from the look on your face that you haven't
forgotten yet—not completely."

"Maybe I haven't forgotten what happened," she
admitted, pulling herself together. "But I've learned to
deal with it. I'm here now, and I'll do everything I can
to help you keep your land." She smiled bravely. "With
my background in accounting, I might be able to find
a solution. John used to claim that it was my creative
number-crunching that put his winery on the national
market."

Her father laughed, the sound rusty from disuse. "I
always thought he got the better part of that deal."

Liana smiled at him. "Spoken like a true father. In
fact, John did more for me than you'll ever know." *Like
trying to show me that there could be a gentle side to
sexual intimacy.* She quelled the wayward thought and
continued brightly, "Now, why don't you tell me exactly what your situation is, here."

THAT NIGHT, AS SHE tossed and turned for hours in the
room she'd once shared with Serena, Liana tried to
come to terms with what she'd learned from her father.

Although the picture he'd painted hadn't been optimistic, she had a sinking feeling that he hadn't told her everything. The fact that Castillo's Arabians was in deep financial trouble was a foregone conclusion. What she still didn't know was *how* deep the trouble ran. Worst of all, she now had a clear image of how it had happened, and she didn't like what she saw.

Frank Castillo was a wizened caricature of the dynamic man he'd once been. The beginning of his decline could be traced to the night of the accident. His daughter Serena had been killed and Liana had run away, leaving him to face his grief alone. Even though Liana knew she might never have recovered if she hadn't left, she couldn't suppress a wave of remorse at the thought of her father struggling all alone to handle his own anguish, in addition to running the ranch.

Her guilt deepened when she remembered how he'd always found time to visit her at least once a year, without ever asking that she reciprocate.

"Now it looks as if I may have come too late," she whispered to herself. The problem was, she didn't have that much free capital to offer. Almost everything she owned was tied up in the winery in Oregon. Restlessly, she got up and went to stare out the window, holding the yellowed lace curtain aside with one hand. Pale moonlight illuminated the yard below, and the distant paddock, softening the signs of age and neglect. It had been such a lovely place, once.... She straightened with sudden resolve. Maybe things looked hopeless at the moment, but she wasn't going to give up. Not yet. Her father deserved more than that from her.

LIANA PLACED HER HANDS on her hips and surveyed the results of four hours' hard work in the once-grimy kitchen. The cabinets looked almost white again, the old linoleum floor shone with a new layer of wax, and the windows were crystal clear, if curtainless. The old gingham fabric hadn't survived a trip through the washing machine. No matter, she decided; she'd buy new ones when she went into town to get groceries. As far as she could tell, her father had been existing almost entirely on canned and frozen food—and the awful honey wine he made. He'd insisted she try some last night, and her stomach still felt queasy.

"Looks good in here," her father announced from the doorway. "Better than it has for a long time."

Liana smiled and tucked a few wayward strands of hair into the French braid that hung halfway down her back. "Thanks. Could you give me a lift to town? I need to get some things, and I'm not sure I can handle that old pickup of yours." Actually, after he'd met her at the airport the day before yesterday, she'd wondered if the decrepit old thing would make the trip home.

"I'll be glad to take you, but it'll have to wait awhile. This morning I found a big puddle of hydraulic fluid under the damned thing, and I can't drive it anywhere until I make sure the brakes work." Frank crossed the room, opened a drawer and began rummaging around. "Before I do that, though, I have to finish grooming Sonny. I just came up to get my hoof knife." He found it and started back out the door, calling over his shoulder, "His hooves need trimming, but that shouldn't take too long."

"There's no rush." Liana followed him outside and over to the paddock where she perched on a rail to watch. Sonny stood in the middle of the enclosure, his head crosstied between two posts. Her father ran a reassuring hand over the horse's gleaming neck before stooping to pick up one hoof. With his back to the horse's head, he propped the hoof between his knees and proceeded to trim it.

Liana knew the process well. She'd done it many times herself, and most horses didn't mind at all. But she still didn't like the idea of her father doing it to an excitable animal like Sonny. Biting her lip, she kept an eye on Sonny's ears, a good indicator of a horse's mood. She needn't have worried. Sonny appeared unconcerned about the whole process.

She allowed herself to relax a bit and enjoy the peaceful setting. It was quiet enough for her to hear the occasional buzz of an insect as it zoomed by. But the tranquillity was suddenly shattered by a snort and then a frightened squeal from Sonny.

As she watched in horror, the stallion tried to rear but was restrained by the ropes. Then his massive hindquarters lurched, knocking her father to the ground and into the path of Sonny's wildly stomping hooves. Heart pounding, Liana jumped off the fence and raced forward. But before she could do anything, her father cried out in agony and grabbed for his leg.

Liana screamed, "Dad!" and slapped Sonny's rump with all her might. When the frenzied horse jumped aside in surprise, she grasped her father under his arms and, with a strength bolstered by pumping adrenaline, hauled him to safety a few yards away.

He groaned and rolled to his side, clutching his injured leg. Liana knelt beside him, trying to keep the panic out of her voice. "Dad, can you tell where you're hurt? Is it just your leg?"

He nodded and gasped, "Just the leg... Pretty sure... it's broken."

Liana felt the icy calm of shock begin to settle over her. When she spoke this time, she managed to sound calm. "Then don't try to sit up or even move. I'm going to go call an ambulance."

She started to get up, but he grabbed her hand. "No! No ambulance."

"But we have to get you to a hospital. We can't take the pickup if the brakes aren't working. Besides, I'm not sure I could drive it."

Her father's face was as pale as death, but his mouth was set stubbornly. "No ambulance. Can't afford it."

"But the insurance will—" She stopped as another distressing thought occurred to her. "You do have insurance, don't you?"

He shook his head and avoided her eyes. "Didn't think I needed it."

Which translated to "couldn't afford it," she thought dismally.

"Guess that wasn't such good thinkin'," he went on painfully, "since someone is obviously out to get me."

"Out to get you? What are you talking about?"

"Someone was shooting at me."

"Shooting!" Incredulous, Liana stared at him. "Whatever makes you think that? There weren't any gunshots."

Her father grunted. "Probably used a silencer. Heard something whiz past my head and hit the dirt. Next thing I knew, Sonny went crazy." He paused, breathing heavily, then added, "Must've gotten him in the flank, from the way he jumped."

Liana looked at the horse, who was still snorting and yanking at the ropes that restrained him. There didn't appear to be a mark on him. Good grief, was her father hallucinating? "Look, you need a doctor's care. That's all I'm concerned about right now. Don't worry about paying for the ambulance, we'll work something out." Her father began to protest, but her attention was snagged by the sound of a motor. When she got up to look, she saw a black Toyota pickup, its bed enclosed by a custom-made shell, coming up the long drive that connected with the main road.

"Oh, damn," her father moaned. "That's Valentin. Get him off my property."

Just what I don't need, Liana thought, starting for the paddock gate. By the time she got there, Max had parked and was walking toward her.

"No matter what you're here for, I don't have time," she said, intending to walk right past him and on to the house. He caught her arm, forcing her to stop.

"Hey, wait a minute. I was just returning these." He held out her sandals, looking annoyed, but his expression sharpened to concern when his gaze slid past her to her father's prone figure. "What happened?" he demanded, dropping the sandals as he strode past her into the paddock.

Irritated, she followed. "Something spooked Sonny and he trampled on Dad. I'm afraid his leg might be broken, but you needn't worry yourself. I was just on my way to call an ambulance."

Max knelt down beside her father who growled, "Get away from me, Valentin. I don't need your help."

Ignoring the insult, Max asked, "Can you move it at all?"

The two men stared each other down for what seemed an eternity before her father snarled, "No. Are you happy now?"

"Not in the least," Max replied, rising. To Liana he added, "You'd better call that ambulance. I'll wait here with him."

"No blasted ambulance!" her father exclaimed, breaking off in another groan. Max glanced at Liana inquiringly.

"He can't . . ." she began, then pride stopped her.

Max seemed to evaluate the situation for a moment, then nodded, as if he understood. "All right. We'll take him in my truck. It'll probably be faster than waiting for the ambulance, anyway. He can ride in back with his leg stretched out. I'll look in the stable and see if I can find something to use as a stretcher. Liana, go get some blankets to cushion his leg. . . ."

Liana wavered only a moment. Max might have his faults, but it appeared as if he were offering genuine help in a time of dire need. Only a fool would refuse that.

When she returned a short while later with the blankets, a makeshift splint held her father's injured leg straight, and he was cursing eloquently as Max gently maneuvered him onto a wide plank of wood.

Max spared her only a glance before asking, "Do you think you can handle the end by his feet?"

She nodded, and bent to grasp the plank. Between them, they carried her father to the open gate of the pickup where they slid him in, board and all. By the time they had him propped up inside with the blankets cushioning his leg, he was gray-faced from the pain, but he found enough breath to wheeze, "Sonny."

Liana groaned. They couldn't just leave the animal crosstied in the hot sun. On the other hand, she wasn't sure what he'd do if she untied him.

"Don't worry, I'll take care of him," Max offered unexpectedly.

"No, wait!" Liana called out, but he evidently didn't hear her as he walked quickly toward the paddock. She could only watch in amazement as he confidently approached the nervous stallion. The horse snorted, his ears swiveling backward, then to the front as Max came around to face him. They stood there for a timeless moment, man and beast sizing each other up, as Max spoke in a slow, mesmerizing drawl. Then he began to stroke the proud stallion's neck.

A grudging respect stole over Liana as she looked on. She could almost feel the calming power of Max's hands as he reassured the animal. Within minutes, the horse was allowing himself to be led to the stable.

"Miserable beast," her father muttered. "First he nearly stomps me to death, then he allows my worst enemy to lead him around like a puppy. Son of the Sheik's the wrong name for him. He should have been called Son of a B—"

"Dad!" Liana interjected sharply, her reverie broken. "Let it go. I know you're in pain, but getting upset isn't going to help." She scooted in beside him. "I'm going to sit back here with you, so you won't slide around."

When he returned from the stable, Max noted the seating arrangement and nodded in approval. "Hang in there, Frank. I'll try to avoid as many bumps as possible."

Liana's father started to snarl a response, but she quelled him with a look as Max shut the tailgate.

The drive to the hospital seemed endless to Liana. She breathed a deep sigh of relief when Max finally pulled into the driveway of a modest-size structure that looked brand-new and ultramodern. The area looked familiar to her, but the hospital had obviously been constructed long after she'd left Temecula.

Almost at once, hospital attendants appeared to whisk her father off to Emergency, leaving Liana to fill out the numerous forms required for admittance. As she turned to look for a seat in the Emergency waiting room, she nearly bumped into Max. "You don't have to stay any longer," she said, even though she couldn't deny a tug of reluctance at the thought of his leaving. Although he'd remained quietly in the background up to that point, she'd felt his reassuring presence and was grateful for it. "I can't begin to thank you—"

"Forget that, for now," he interrupted, guiding her toward two empty chairs. "I'll stay and help you with the paperwork."

Reluctantly, she accepted Max's offer of help, but after the forms were completed, she again told him he didn't have to stay. "The nurse said the X rays and everything could take a long time."

Max shook his head. "I don't have anything to do that can't wait. Besides, how would you get back to the ranch?"

She shrugged. "I'll figure something out. In fact, if my father has to stay here for a while, I suppose I'll have to lease a car. I don't trust that old truck of his."

"I have a Honda Civic hatchback you could use. It's not new, but it's reliable."

Astonishment floored her for a moment. "Why would you want to do that? I mean, I really appreciate all you've done so far, but…a car? Isn't that a bit much, considering that we're practically enemies?"

Max's dark brows lowered reprovingly. "Now you sound like your father." He leaned forward, crowding her a bit. "Did it ever occur to you that I might be offering my help because it's the neighborly thing to do? Temecula may have grown a great deal since you left, but those of us who've lived here for a while still believe in helping each other when there's trouble."

Realizing how churlish she'd sounded, Liana muttered, "Sorry," and glanced down at her hands. "I guess I just don't know what to believe at this point," she continued. "Nothing's as I expected it to be—the ranch, my father..." Without warning, tears choked her as the strain of the afternoon took its toll.

"Don't worry about it," Max said quickly. "I realize you're under a lot of stress, worrying about your dad." His warm hand covered hers briefly. "You look as if you could use a cup of coffee. Why don't we go find the cafeteria in this place?"

Blinking back tears, she glanced toward the emergency-room door. "What if they need me for something?"

"We'll tell the nurse where we're going and check back here periodically, if you like." He gave her hands a little squeeze. "Come on. The change of scenery will do you good."

She finally agreed, and they followed the nurse's directions to the cafeteria, which turned out to be a spartan room with a bank of vending machines against one wall. On the opposite side, floor-to-ceiling windows overlooked a tiny garden. She opted for a canned soda and he selected an orange juice. They sat down across from each other at a table next to the windows, and although there were a few hospital employees at nearby tables, Liana suddenly felt uncomfortable. With such a small distance separating her from Max, she was forced to confront his potent attractiveness, and she didn't like the way it made her feel. No man should look that good, she thought, noting the speculative glances they were receiving from the women in the room. At a loss for words, she feigned an interest in the miniature palms and flowering cactus outside, until Max's voice drew her back.

"So, tell me about Oregon."

She raised her eyebrows questioningly. "Why in the world would you want to hear about that?"

"Because I think you need to get your mind off of your father for a while. Also, you told me yesterday that the local gossip about you is all wrong, and I'd like to hear the truth. What have you been doing since you left here?"

LIANA TOOK A SIP of her cola to settle the little twist of unease in her stomach. She didn't enjoy talking about herself. "There isn't much to tell, really. I went to live with my aunt Opal—she's my father's sister. I attended college, became an accountant, and got married. Nothing unusual or terribly interesting."

Max's expression tightened perceptibly, his gaze straying to her ring finger, which was bare. "You're married? I didn't know that."

"*Was* married," she corrected. "My husband died two years ago."

"That must've been tough."

Liana turned to look at the garden again. "Yes, it was. There was an accident at the winery." She could still remember the numbing emptiness she'd felt when they'd come and told her.

"He worked for a winery?" Max's voice rose in surprise.

She shook her head. "He owned one. Ever hear of Liebhardt's?"

"Of course! They went to national distribution a few years back. It caused a lot of talk at the local Vintners' Association meeting, because Liebhardt's seemed to appear out of nowhere."

She smiled sadly. "That we did. Of course, there was a lot of work involved, and considerable risks, but John was never afraid of taking chances." He'd certainly taken one on her, although she knew that one hadn't paid off as well as he'd expected. The thought saddened her.

"You obviously cared a great deal for him," Max said quietly. "Are you in charge of the winery now?"

She shook her head and looked up at him. "No. That's in the capable hands of John's son, Eric." When she saw the confusion on Max's face she smiled. "No, not my son. John was older than me and had been married before. In fact, his children are almost as old as I am."

"So, what have you been doing since your husband died?" Max persisted.

She shrugged and ran a fingertip around the rim of the soda can. "Oh, I've continued in my capacity as accountant for the winery, but mostly I've tried to stay out of the way of Eric and his new wife." What she didn't add was that lately, even though they all got along quite well, she'd been feeling more and more like a third wheel, living in the same house with them.

"Eric is very good at running the place. Which is why I didn't feel too guilty about hiring a substitute accountant when my father called for help. Although, if

I'd had any idea of the trouble he was having, I would've come sooner."

The door to the cafeteria swung open, and the emergency-room nurse summoned them, forestalling any further conversation. "The doctor wants to see you," she explained. Her gaze was glued admiringly on Max as they accompanied her down the hall. When he noticed, he responded with a boyish grin, and the woman nearly melted.

Even in the midst of her distress, Liana felt a pinprick of annoyance. Max might claim he'd changed, but it sure looked like the old "heartbreaker" charm was still as potent as ever.

However, she forgot Max and his admirer as soon as they reached the doctor's consulting room. The news wasn't good. Frank's leg was fractured in several places and would require traction. As Liana listened with growing dismay, the doctor explained that her father might require a lengthy stay in the hospital.

"How long?" she inquired anxiously.

"We'll have to decide on a day-to-day basis," the doctor replied. "His general physical condition isn't what it should be. If you like, you can see him as soon as we finish with the cast."

Later, while Max waited in the lobby, Liana stood in her father's hospital room gazing down at his gaunt face. He'd been sedated, but when she touched his hand, his eyes slowly opened. "Liana . . . Sorry, honey. I shouldn't have dragged you into this." He drew a labored breath. "Guess it's all over now. I'll never be able to fight him from a hospital bed."

Frank Castillo had never been a quitter, and the fact that he seemed to be giving up now distressed Liana greatly. What would he do if he lost the ranch? Give up on life, too? She couldn't allow that to happen.

"Don't worry, Dad," she said firmly. "I'm still here, and if it's at all possible, you'll get to keep your land."

He shook his head wearily. "No, you shouldn't get involved. Valentin got me today, he might try to hurt you next. I should have thought of that before I sent for you. Go home, Liana. Go back to Oregon where you'll be safe."

"Absolutely not," she pronounced. "And what's all this nonsense about Max getting you? He wasn't even around when Sonny went berserk."

"You don't have to be close with a gun."

Liana tried to hang on to her patience. "Dad, the idea of someone lurking around taking shots at you—with a silenced gun, no less—sounds like something out of a spy movie." She leaned over to kiss his lined cheek and attempted a teasing grin. "Know what I think? I think it was a horsefly, or one of those darn bees you keep. As excitable as Sonny is, I'll bet even an insect bite would be enough to set him off."

"You don't know Max Valentin," her father insisted.

"Maybe not, but I do know Sonny. His temperament seems meaner than Max's, so far. Now, you get some rest, and I'll be back to see you soon."

When she joined Max in the lobby, he suggested that they drive back to his place so she could pick up the car he'd offered. "That is, if you've decided to use it," he added, with a wry smile.

She hesitated, remembering her father's warning. But she saw no sign of guile in Max's eyes. Besides, Max *had* gone out of his way to be helpful. "All right, I will," she said, finally. "But I can't understand why you want to help me when I still intend to fight you any way I can for my father's land."

Max appeared to weigh that, then let his gaze ride slowly down over her rumpled blouse and worn jeans. His eyes had a sardonic glint when they met hers again. "Maybe I just like the way you look in a wet T-shirt," he said quietly, then turned and walked out the door.

Scarcely believing what she'd heard, Liana remained frozen for almost a minute, before she gathered her wits and charged out after him.

3

BY THE TIME LIANA reached Max, who was waiting in the parking lot by his truck, she knew exactly what she had to say. Unfortunately, that didn't make saying it any easier. "Mr. Valentin," she began seriously.

"Mrs. Liebhardt," he rallied, straight-faced.

"It's Ms. Castillo. I think we need to have an understanding about our relationship."

He raised an eyebrow. "I didn't know we had one, but please go on. I'm intrigued."

He'd purposely misinterpreted her. "We don't have one," she agreed tightly. "And I intend for it to stay that way. I won't accept any more of your help if you think you can—"

"Purchase your affections?" he supplied helpfully. "The thought never occurred to me."

"Then why did you make that comment about my...uh...T-shirt?"

"Because I was tired of having you assume that my offers of help are somehow connected with the land I want to reclaim. I thought sex would be a refreshing change." He indicated the truck with a wave of his hand. "Now that we have that settled, can we go?"

As he stood there with the breeze ruffling the thick waves of his ebony hair, Liana came to the depressing realization that he'd probably never had to purchase any woman's affections. But she refused to back down. "We can go—as long as you don't forget what I said," she agreed finally.

"Absolutely, Ms. Castillo." Max lowered his head in mock subservience as she climbed up into the seat. After he'd gotten in on the driver's side he added, "By the way, why didn't you change it?"

She glanced at him, confused. "Change what?"

"Your last name, when you got married." He started the truck and pulled out of the parking lot onto the main road. "You said your husband was a lot older than you, which means he came from a generation that believed a wife should take her husband's name. I just wondered how he felt about you keeping your maiden name."

Again, Liana knew a moment of disquiet. Why all the questions about her personal life? Still, it was a fairly tame subject, compared to wet T-shirts. "John was a very kind man," she began reluctantly. "He understood that, as my father's only surviving child, I wanted to keep the family name."

"But what if you'd had children? Whose name would they have been given?"

She shrugged and turned to look at an orange grove they were passing. "That was a moot point. We chose not to have children."

"Funny, I always pictured you as the type who'd have a bunch of kids."

She sent him a sharp glance. "What makes you think you're such an authority on me? We haven't seen each other for fourteen years."

"Yeah, but I know how you were when we were kids. You always had a soft spot for babies of any kind. Remember when my dad ran sheep? Every lambing season, you'd be underfoot, petting them, giving them names." He chuckled softly. "Then there was the time you caught Rennie tormenting the barn cat's kittens. You were such a shy little mouse normally, none of us could believe the shiner you gave him."

Liana gave in to a rueful smile. "He was twelve and I was only ten." Her smile faded. "I don't think he ever quite forgave me for it." Her smile faded.

"Hey, what happened?" Max inquired softly. "For a minute there, I had you smiling."

"You did. But I can't—I don't like to think about that time of my life too much. Could we talk about something else?"

"All right. What are your plans now that your father's out of commission? Do you still intend to help him exercise his option to buy my land?" As he spoke, he turned the truck into a driveway marked by a large, ornately lettered sign that read: Valentin Winery— Tours And Tasting Room Open Daily 10:00 a.m.-5:00 p.m.

The winery and the Valentin residences stood about a half mile away on the crest of a hill. The area held numerous smaller hills covered with row after row of carefully staked grapevines.

Liana sat a little straighter, gathering her resolve again. "I'm going to try. A lot depends on what I find when I go through his financial records. He and I were planning to do that this evening. Now, I guess I'll have to do it myself."

"I don't think you'll like what you find," Max warned. "Who's going to run the ranch? Even with only four horses to care for, there's a lot of work."

"I'll manage somehow," she said firmly. "Don't bother trying to discourage me. I'm not afraid of hard work." Of course, she wasn't used to real physical labor anymore, but she wouldn't let that stop her.

As he guided the truck up to the private parking area beside the main house, Max uttered a low "Hmm" that could have been construed as disbelief, but Liana chose to ignore it. Instead she turned her attention to the impressive assortment of buildings that had been added since she'd last seen the place. The barn had been replaced by two large rectangular buildings, and just to the north of them was a small structure done in the Spanish style of the two residences. Over the door hung another ornate sign that read, Tasting Room. It all looked so professional and efficient, compared to the small, part-time operation Max's father had run.

"I had no idea...." She shook her head, incredulous. "You've done so much."

"There've been some big changes since I returned from France," Max admitted. "I plan to do a lot more, if a certain stubborn rancher will see reason." He got out of the truck and came around to open her door. "Would you like the grand tour?"

That was the last thing she wanted at the moment. Seeing the obvious signs of Max's success only made her father's failure seem more inevitable. "I really don't have time," she said, checking her watch. "I have a lot to do today."

She thought she saw a flash of disappointment in his eyes, but he nodded. "Another time, then. Come on, the Honda's parked behind my place."

To her surprise, he started toward the smaller house. "You live here?" she asked, as they circled the building.

"Yes. Sybille has the main house. We find this arrangement allows each of us more…privacy." He spoke without rancor, but his jaw tightened, reminding Liana of the animosity there'd been between him and his stepmother years ago. Was that the real reason behind the separate residences? Or was it because of the endless line of women who supposedly paraded through his life?

Nettled by the latter possibility, she chose to wait outside while he went into the kitchen to fetch a spare set of car keys. When he returned, she followed him to the silver Honda Civic parked in an old storage shed.

The car was a little dusty, but when Max got in and started the engine, it hummed evenly. After backing the vehicle out of the shed, he got out and motioned her to the driver's seat with a sweeping gesture. "It's all yours. If you have any problems with it, just call me."

She started to get in, then turned to look at him. "Are you sure you want to do this?" she inquired uncertainly. "It seems like you're sabotaging your own plans by helping me."

Amusement sparkled in his eyes. "It'll take more than the loan of a car for you to pull off what you're attempting."

Unsure how she should respond to that, she simply said, "Well . . . thanks anyway." She slipped behind the wheel and let him push the door shut behind her. But before she drove off, she rolled down the window and added, "I'll think of a way to pay you back—you can count on that."

Max smiled enigmatically. "I'm sure you will."

Liana put the car in gear and drove off, but on the way back to the ranch, she began to wonder about the meaning behind his last words. What made him so sure she'd be able to repay him? For that matter, what did she have to offer? She would probably need every bit of spare money she could scrounge just to bail her father out, if that were possible. Repaying this debt would take some creative thinking, she decided.

SHE WAS STILL THINKING about possible remunerations the following morning as she sat down to sort through the jumble of papers on her father's huge rolltop desk. By noon, paying Max back for the use of his car was the least of her worries. Everywhere she looked, she found financial ruin. Bills had gone unpaid for months, the balance in her father's checking account was nearly zero, and his savings had long ago disappeared. Worse yet, he was at least two payments behind on the lease, and the limit named in the default clause was three months.

"Which you've obviously known all along, haven't you, Max Valentin?" she muttered angrily, shoving away from the desk. No wonder he felt he could afford to be magnanimous—even to the extent of loaning her his car. He figured she didn't have a chance against him. Grabbing the car keys and her purse, she headed for the door. She wasn't admitting defeat—there still might be ways to stop him. But, given the circumstances, she wasn't going to continue using his blasted car.

A few minutes later, she pulled into the winery parking lot with a screech of tires that drew the attention of several visitors who were walking toward their own cars. Ignoring their stares, she marched into the tasting room and startled a young maintenance man by demanding to know the whereabouts of his employer. Directed to the fermenting building next door, she headed over there, still in high dudgeon.

She came to an abrupt halt, however, when she flung open the door and encountered Max in the midst of a group of stylishly dressed women. They were gazing up at a huge stainless-steel fermenting tank as Max's rich voice rumbled on about yeast lees and vintages. His crisp white shirt was unbuttoned just far enough to offer a tantalizing glimpse of dark chest hair, and the sleeves were rolled up to reveal muscular lightly tanned forearms. The snowy whiteness of the material made his eyes look impossibly blue, and his perfectly tailored black slacks showcased the tight physique of a runner.

Suddenly remembering the well-worn jeans and faded tank top she'd donned that morning to do chores, Liana felt at a disadvantage.

Max never missed a beat in his smooth discourse, but his gaze locked onto her with such intensity, several of the women glanced her way, eyebrows raised. Mortified, Liana turned to go, but heard him quickly say, "Now, ladies, if you'll excuse me, I have an urgent meeting with a business associate. The tasting room is open, if you'd like to sample some of our wines."

As she half jogged away, Liana could have sworn she heard a collective sigh of disappointment from his audience. Madder than ever, she started back toward the Honda, intending to leave the keys in it before she walked home. But Max caught up with her before she'd gone halfway across the parking lot.

"Liana, wait," he said, trying to grab her. She dodged his hand, but she wasn't quick enough to avoid the strong arm that wrapped around her waist, swinging her up and around.

When her feet touched the ground again, she turned on him furiously. "What do you think you're doing?"

"I was about to ask you that, but judging from the look on your face, I don't think I want to hear your answer out here." He glanced significantly at the women exiting the fermenting building, then took her arm. "Come on, we'll go to my office."

"I'm not going anywhere with you." She tried to pull away from him, but he wouldn't let go.

"I'd reconsider, if I were you." Some of those women are quite prominent in this town. Were you thinking of providing them with some hot luncheon gossip?"

Gossip. That hated word stopped her as nothing else could have. Max seemed to realize he'd gotten through to her, because he started toward the tasting-room building, still gripping her arm.

Seeing the direction he was headed in, Liana began to dig in her heels. "I can't go in there—"

"Relax," he interrupted, guiding her around the back of the structure to a set of stairs. At the top was a door marked Private. When he opened it, the cool blast of air-conditioning rushed out to meet them. Reluctantly, Liana stepped inside and discovered she was in a modest, tasteful office. Max led her straight across to an inner door, which opened into to a slightly larger office— obviously his. Here the decor was more manly, with a large oak desk and black leather chairs. He seated her in one, then perched before her on the edge of the desk, his long legs stretched out and crossed at the ankles.

"Now, why do I get the impression you'd like to feed me into one of my crushing machines?"

He looked so perfectly masculine, so supremely confident, Liana wanted to hit him. "That would be too good an end for a sneaky underhanded person like you," she snapped.

"I see. What sneaky underhanded thing have I done?"

"As if you didn't know." She jumped up to negate the advantage their positions had given him. "I went through my father's papers today, and guess what I found? He's almost three months in arrears in his lease payments." Propping her hands on her hips, she glared at him. "Very clever, Max, letting him get behind like that. All you'd have to do is act on the default clause at the end of the third month." She pushed her face aggressively close to his. "Except for one complication. I'm here now, and the first thing I'm going to do is catch up on those payments." Grabbing her purse, she pawed through it until she found her checkbook. "In fact, I'll write the check now." She quickly scribbled the date and Max's name, then glanced toward him. "Let's see. Three months at—"

"Four," he corrected in a dangerously quiet voice.

Pen poised, she froze. "What?"

"Four months. That's how far behind he is."

Liana felt as if she'd received a blow to the midsection. *Four months?* But that meant . . . She sat down abruptly, the finality of the realization sapping her strength. Why hadn't her father told her? Or was he so far gone, he didn't know himself? His records were in a terrible mess. "Does my father know?" she asked faintly.

"I doubt it. He's still talking about buying out at the end of the lease." Max's eyes narrowed assessingly. "You look a little pale. Hang on and I'll get you something cold to drink." He got up and went to the oak shelving unit that filled one wall. At his touch, one of the cabinet doors opened to reveal a small refrigerator. From it he withdrew a tall greenish-gold wine bottle. With a few economical movements, he uncorked it and poured a small glass of the pale liquid, then returned to hand it to her.

Still dazed, she accepted the slender glass and took a sip. At first the chilled wine merely nipped her taste buds, startling her into awareness. But then she took another taste, letting the flavor blossom on her tongue. Even though she'd never considered her palate to be more than moderately educated, the effect was dazzling. Thanks to John's instruction, she knew something about quality wine, and this was the best sauvignon blanc she'd ever tasted.

Max made a gruff sound of approval. "Well, at least that brought some color back to your cheeks."

"Is this one of yours?" she asked, automatically raising the glass to study the clarity of its contents.

"That is the pride and joy of the Valentin winery, and the foundation for my plans to expand to national distribution."

She lowered the glass and sighed. "Which brings us to the question of why you haven't claimed default on my father's lease and booted him off the land." Her chin rose a bit in challenge. "And why did you let me go on thinking there was any chance of stopping you?"

"I didn't think I should be the one to tell you." Max shrugged and got up to pour himself a glass of the wine. "As for your father," he continued, returning to his place on the edge of the desk, "this may sound strange, but I'd rather not be thought of as the ogre who took his land away from him, even though he obviously can't handle the place anymore. Contrary to what your father may have told you, I've never harbored any animosity toward your family. I thought it might be easier on him—that he might be more resigned to things—if I let him stay until the lease ran out."

Thoroughly perplexed by this unexpected benevolence, Liana asked, "But what about me? Aren't you concerned about the possibility that I might help him keep the land?"

Max gave her a long, assessing look before answering. "Frankly, I don't think you can, but there's something about you that makes me want to give you the chance. You're not like any accountant I've ever known, Liana. Accountants are supposed to be boring and pedantic, but you're all passion and bravado. I find that intriguing."

Passion? She nearly laughed aloud. No one had ever accused her of being passionate. Quite the opposite, actually. True, she'd lost her temper more times than was usual for her since she'd arrived in Temecula, but simple anger and frustration weren't the same as passion. Passion led to pain and destruction.

"Liana." He spoke her name quietly, summoning her back from the edge of dark memories. "Did I say something to upset you?"

She straightened and cleared her throat. "Not exactly. Although, you're wrong about the passion part." She brought the wineglass to her lips and savored the pleasant effect of the complex flavors against her tongue. The wine had a seductive power, just like the man who'd made it, she thought. A short while ago, she'd been furious with him—now, she caught herself almost liking him.

"Not passionate, hmm? I think you're misjudging yourself, but only time will tell." He stood, setting aside his nearly full glass. "Now, since you seem to like my wine so much, would you like to see where it's made?"

Her first instinct was to refuse. After all, they were still on opposite sides as far as the issue of her father's land went. But Max had been more than accommodating about the late payments. On top of that, because of her involvement with the wine-making industry, she had a great deal of professional curiosity about his operation.

"All right," she said, setting her half-empty glass down. "But first let me give you the money for those late payments." She knew the check would take a big bite out of her savings, but she was determined to make the gesture.

He waited patiently as she wrote in the amount and signed her name. When she handed the check to him, he tossed it negligently onto his desk and motioned for her to precede him to the door.

What she saw on their brief tour impressed her. Although not on a scale with the corporate-owned wineries, Max's production seemed to be run with a high level of efficiency. There were areas that could be improved, parts of the process that could be handled more economically, things that she and John had discovered the hard way in their own operation. But the potential for expansion was there, and if the rest of Max's wines were as good as the one she'd tasted, he could do quite well on the national market.

She told him as much as they stepped out into the bright sunshine.

A gleam of pride lit his eyes. "Taste them, and judge for yourself," he challenged, touching her arm as if to lead her toward the tasting room.

She shook her head and glanced down at her work clothes. "I can't. Not dressed like this."

"I don't know . . ." he said, surveying her outfit with a half smile. "On you, I think the ranch-hand look has a certain charm. But if it bothers you, there's a side entrance to the storage area where we can sample in private."

The idea of doing anything private with a man like Max Valentin struck her as being unwise, but before she could say no again, he added, "Come on, it won't take long. And I'd really like your opinion." He gestured expansively. "Consider it payment for the use of my car."

She broke into startled laughter. "My opinion isn't worth that much."

"It is to me," he replied. When he urged her forward again, she didn't resist.

The storage room's cool, dim interior made her shiver at first, but she felt better once her eyes adjusted to the lack of light. Rows of boxes took up half of the room; the other half had wine racks filled with endless bottles, each bearing the distinctive gold-embossed Valentin label and cork seal.

Max excused himself to go get the wine, and Liana wandered up and down the aisles between the racks.

She completed her tour of the room just as he reappeared, loaded down with bottles and glasses. "Come over here," he said, indicating a small table set between two folding chairs in the corner. He poured a little of the first wine into two glasses and handed her one. The expectation in his eyes as he watched her take a sip, nearly made her smile.

The wine was lovely—a light, clean Chardonnay that finished smoothly on her tongue. She nodded her approval. "Very nice. Top quality, in fact."

Max broke into a smile of such incandescent delight it flashed across her senses like lightning, making her feel as if she'd just downed a whole bottle of wine instead of a tiny sip. His smile had the power to seduce in an instant, obliterating common sense and reason. *The smile of a heartbreaker,* she thought. Then, as she stared transfixed, his expression altered. The smile slowly faded and his eyes seemed to darken. He leaned closer until she could see nothing but the intense azure of his eyes. She knew what was coming but, like a moth mesmerized by a flame, she couldn't summon the will to resist.

"Liana..." he murmured the instant before their lips met. A dizzying shock wave of sensation swept through her, sending her back to another time, another kiss. . . .

She'd been fourteen and foolishly in love then, and Max had seemed to epitomize everything she wanted. Unfortunately, being five years her senior, he hadn't seen her as anything more than the shy, skinny kid he'd known since childhood. She hadn't stood a chance against the older, more sophisticated girls who'd chased after him through high school and junior college. But the day Max's grandmother died, everything changed.

Marcelle Valentin had taken over the job of mothering Max when his own mother had died. Everyone knew that when his father had returned from France with his ill-chosen new wife and stepson, Marce had been the stabilizing force in Max's life. Understandably, her death had devastated him....

Liana found him, two days after the funeral, sitting under the low-hanging branches of one of the oaks bordering the pond, his head buried in his arms. Compassion tearing her heart, she quietly sat down next to him, her side almost, but not quite, touching his. When his head jerked up in alarm, she gingerly draped one thin arm across his broad shoulders and whispered, "I...I'm so sorry, Max."

She'd intended only to offer comfort, so it felt like the most natural thing in the world when he scooped her onto his lap and hugged her fiercely. When he tipped his head back, tragedy etched on his handsome young face, and said, "She was the only person in the world who really loved me," Liana's normal reserve shattered.

Taking his face between her hands, she said without thinking, "I love you, Max." Then, on sheer impulse, she kissed him with all the youthful fervor she could muster. She sensed his surprise, his hesitation, and then he started kissing her back, his mouth moving over hers avidly tasting...seeking...giving her pleasure beyond anything she'd ever known— But as quickly as it had begun, it ended. Since her hands were clutching his shoulders, she felt the exact instant his body tensed with the shocking realization of what was happening. Before she could say or do anything, he was shoving her away, turning his back on her, telling her, "Get lost, kid."

Recoiling from the memory, Liana snapped back to the present and the dismaying knowledge that his kiss hadn't lost any of its power over the years. If anything, it had grown stronger, she thought, pulling away from the gentle pressure of his mouth. The kiss he'd just given her had been a simple, undemanding caress. Yet, she felt as overwhelmed and shaken as she had fourteen years ago.

"Why..." she began, then nervously cleared her throat. "Why did you do that?"

He grinned and shrugged. "Because it seemed appropriate."

For some reason, his nonchalant attitude annoyed her more than any other response could have. "'Appropriate'? Is that your only criteria for kissing a woman? If so, I can understand how you've maintained your reputation as a heartbreaker."

Max's expression darkened. "I told you once before not to give too much credence to the gossip you hear. Besides, it was meant as a friendly gesture, nothing more."

Again, his apparent dispassion nettled her. "Well, I'd prefer that you not do it again." Crossing her arms over her chest, she sat back in her chair and added, "I'm not interested in that sort of thing, Max."

His gaze sharpened with curiosity. "Care to explain why?"

Suddenly uneasy with the direction of the conversation, she said, "No. Anyway, I think I've had enough wine."

"How could that be?" he demanded, astonished. "You've hardly had any. That amount shouldn't have affected you. Unless . . ." He regarded her uncertainly. "Do you have a problem with alcohol?"

She attempted a light laugh. "No. I'm just—I think I should be getting back to the ranch. There's still so much to be done."

Max studied her for a moment, his gaze locked with hers as if he were trying to read her thoughts. Then he nodded slowly. "All right. We'll finish the tasting another time."

Anxious to escape the disturbing magnetism that seemed to pull her toward him, she stood up too quickly, nearly tipping her chair over. Immediately he reached out to steady her, and the touch of his hands on her bare arms sent a flash of sensation through her, deepening her distress. "I—Thank you for the wine and the tour. You've done amazing things with the place, so far." She pulled away and hurried to the door.

"I plan to do a lot more," he said, following her outside.

She stopped to give him a warning look. "If you're referring to the expansion onto my father's land, nothing's changed in that regard, as far as I'm concerned. I'm still going to help him in any way I can." She dug Max's car keys out of her purse and offered them to him.

"I don't think giving my opinion on a few wines enti-
tles me to the use of your car."

Max refused to take them. "I made the offer and I'm
sticking by it. We may be contending over a piece of
land, but that doesn't mean we have to act like enemies. I think there's been enough animosity between
our families."

Liana weighed her options and realized she didn't
really have many. The large sum of money she'd just
given him to catch up on her father's lease payments
had seriously depleted her funds. Heaven only knew
what kinds of repairs her father's truck would need, and
leasing a car would take money she could be using to
salvage the ranch. Yet, she needed reliable transportation, especially with her father in the hospital. She eyed
Max warily. "If you think being nice to me will change
my mind—"

Max let out an impatient sigh. "I think I know you
well enough by now to realize that won't happen. Take
the car, Liana."

She chewed on her lip a moment before acquiescing.
"All right. But only until I can make other arrange-
ments." She walked the short distance to the car, then
turned back just before getting in. "By the way, thank
you." The inadequacy of those words hounded her as
she drove off. But she couldn't dodge a feeling that she
might regret becoming indebted to him.

Max stood in the parking lot watching the car dis-
appear, his forehead creased in thought. Who would
have believed after all these years that little Liana could
still get him hot with a mere kiss? She'd felt it, too—he

was certain. Back in the storage room, there'd been a sensual undercurrent strong enough to suck the corks out of the bottles racked nearby—just like fourteen years ago. That time, he'd felt compelled to hide his response—because of her youth and innocence. He no longer felt bound by the difference in their ages, and yet, some instinct had warned him to hold back this time, too. So he'd played it cool, reining in his impulse to haul her into his arms and *really* kiss her. Judging by her reaction, he'd made the right decision. For some reason, Liana wasn't ready to admit to the powerful feelings drawing them together, and he didn't think it was due entirely to their opposition over a piece of property.

Footsteps sounded behind him and he pivoted to find Sybille approaching, her mouth curled into a cunning smile. "So you decided to take my advice. Very clever, loaning her your car. Does that mean she's agreed to help you change the old fool's mind?"

Irritation shot through Max at her assumption. "It means she needed transportation," he snapped. "My help doesn't come with a price tag."

Sybille's eyebrows rose in surprise. "But surely, now that her father's in the hospital, she'll see the futility of trying to keep the place."

Max bit back a derisive reply. The situation was more futile than Sybille knew. He'd purposely kept her in the dark about it, knowing she would have been pushing him to throw Frank out the minute he'd fallen behind in his lease payments. "Liana is very loyal to her father," he said. "I admire her for that. She also seems to have a good deal of business sense, and thinks she can bail him out."

"And you're going to just stand by and let her?" Sybille demanded, incensed. "Why, you're even *helping* her by loaning her a car." Her lips curled sarcastically. "If I didn't know you better, I'd think you were the one who's being charmed."

"But that would be my business, not yours." Max glowered at her. "And we don't meddle in each other's business. Right?"

Resentment hardened Sybille's eyes for a moment, but then she molded her features into a look of concern. "I'm only afraid that history will repeat itself," she said. "My poor Rennie and his friend Arlie lost their heads over those Castillo girls, and look what happened to them."

Max doubted his stepbrother or Arlie had been entirely innocent in that incident, but he wasn't inclined to argue the point. "You worry too much," he replied gruffly. "I'm not going to repeat history." At the moment, the only history he wanted to repeat was kissing Liana. He smiled to himself, remembering the unexpected potency of that brief contact.

He turned to gaze in the direction Liana had taken. If a simple kiss could affect him as strongly as the one they'd just shared, what would happen if they made love? Just the thought stirred an elemental hunger in him, and his mouth firmed with resolve. The possibilities were tantalizing, and he intended to explore them fully.

4

LIANA PAUSED TO WIPE the perspiration from her brow and surveyed the discouraging amount of progress she'd made in the past two days. Most of that time she'd spent working in the barn, clearing out useless junk, organizing salvageable items, and the place still looked terrible. Rusting pieces of farm machinery littered the floor; old harnesses and other bits of livery—cracked and dried beyond saving—spilled from sagging boxes. Normally, just maintaining a ranch would have been a daunting prospect to a woman who'd lately spent most of her time sitting at a desk, manipulating facts and figures. But on top of the regular chores involved with caring for the horses, she also faced a huge backlog of cleaning and repairs that needed attention.

"Hello? Anybody home?"

The greeting came so unexpectedly, Liana jumped and dropped the empty liniment bottle she'd been about to discard. She whirled around and saw a tall gangly figure silhouetted against the bright sunlight pouring through the barn's open door. Because her eyes had become accustomed to the dimness inside, she couldn't make out any features, but the unfamiliar voice had definitely been masculine.

She tensed, realizing how isolated and vulnerable she was at the moment. But she refused to give in to panic. Reaching for the rusting pitchfork she'd propped against the wall earlier, she replied as calmly as possible: "I'm back here. Can I help you?"

The figure moved closer, and she saw he had an angular freckled face and pale blond hair that formed an unruly fringe over his forehead. She guessed his age to be early twenties. He was dressed simply, in jeans and a T-shirt that were clean but well-worn. When he stopped a few feet from her and offered a self-conscious smile, it did little to dispel her unease. She forced herself to smile back, but as she did so, she noticed his eyes. Another trickle of apprehension ran down her spine. Something about those eyes bothered her, although she couldn't immediately say why. The irises were an eerie, washed-out blue, and his eyelashes were so pale, they were nearly invisible.

"Hi, I'm Jeff Moser," he said, sticking a hand out for her to shake.

Moser! The name resounded in her mind like a thunderclap, bringing in its wake a flood of unwelcome memories. Memories of another boy named Moser and a night filled with terror and pain. Memories of another pair of pale blue eyes, filled with feral lust—

She jerked out of the memory to realize that Jeff's smile had faltered, and his hand had dropped to his side.

"I see you haven't forgotten the name," he said dryly. "Yes, I'm related to the Arlie Moser you knew. He was my cousin."

Struggling to subdue the dark images that rose up to haunt her, she merely nodded.

Jeff cleared his throat nervously. "I know there was some bad feeling between your family and my relatives after the accident, but it happened so long ago, I thought you might be willing to let bygones be bygones."

Had she reached that point? Liana wondered. Up until the time she'd returned here, she'd believed herself free of the past. But it was harder to maintain that belief when there were so many reminders. For her own benefit as much as for his, she said firmly, "You're right, it was a long time ago. I don't believe in living in the past." She offered him her hand and he grinned as he gave it a hearty shake.

"Now, is there anything I can help you with?" she continued.

"Well, yes." He shrugged and shoved his hands into his back pockets. "I heard about your dad's accident. And I, uh, wondered if you might be looking for some temporary help. I'm due to report to marine boot camp in San Diego in a couple of months, and I'm trying to earn a little money in the meantime to buy some wheels and stuff."

Liana considered his offer. If the Mosers were as unsuccessful at farming as they'd been years ago, she could believe he needed the money. His father, and Arlie's, had seemed to produce kids more easily than crops. But the idea of hiring Jeff—of seeing those eyes on a regular basis—made her stomach tighten.

"I'm not sure I'm in the market for help right now," she hedged. "What kind of work can you do?"

"Anything you need, as long as I can do it in the morning. I've already got a part-time job in the afternoons." He tossed his hands out expansively. "I've helped my dad run the farm for years. And I've had some experience working on cars at the local gas station."

An idea flashed through her mind. If she got her father's truck running properly, she'd be able to return Max's car and end her obligation to him. "How are you at fixing old pickups?"

"Pretty good." A self-deprecating chuckle escaped him. "That seems to be the only kind of truck my family ever owned."

"How much would you charge?" she asked, interested in spite of her reservations about hiring him.

He shrugged again. "Depends on what needs to be done. But I guarantee I'm cheaper than any of those shops in town. If you like, I could take a look at it now."

She hesitated only a moment before agreeing. After all, it wouldn't hurt for him to look. "It's outside," she said, leading the way.

To his credit, Jeff seemed to know his way around vehicles as he crawled over and under the old Chevy pickup. Also, the cost estimate he gave her for the repairs was within reason for her budget. Still, she hesitated, using the excuse of needing references before she made a decision. To her surprise, Jeff mentioned Sybille Valentin as being one of the people he had done odd jobs for in the past.

"In fact," he added, wiping his hands on an old rag he'd found in the cab of the truck. "She's the one who suggested I come over here."

Further astounded, Liana laughed uneasily. "I can't imagine why she'd want to help me. My father claims she still blames me and my sister for the death of her son."

Uncertainty flickered in Jeff's eyes, but he shook his head. "I don't think she feels that way anymore." He gave her an apologetic smile. "From what I hear, your father seems to be the only one hanging on to the old grudge."

That possibility had occurred to Liana, but she wasn't going to admit it. "Regardless, I still want some time to think before I make a decision about having the pickup fixed. I'll call you in a few days. Your parents are still in the directory, aren't they?"

"Yeah. If it'll help you decide, once I get the truck running I can use it to haul away some of that stuff for you." He indicated the barn with a jerk of his head, then sauntered over to the corral where an ancient ten-speed bicycle stood propped. "Unfortunately, these are my only wheels at the moment, so I can't do any hauling right now."

"I'll keep that in mind," she promised as he swung onto the bike and started off down the drive.

BY THE TIME LIANA returned from a visit to her father the next day, she'd nearly decided to go ahead and hire

Jeff. Of course, her father had instantly opposed the
idea when she brought it up.

"You can't trust a Moser," he'd warned. "There's bad
blood in that family. Look what happened to Arlie."
But when she'd asked if Jeff or his family had ever been
in serious trouble, her father couldn't come up with
anything more serious than a little Saturday-night ca-
rousing.

Now, as she parked Max's car under one of the huge
oaks that grew near the house, she came to a decision.
If Jeff's references checked out, she'd hire him. Her
father's inability to let go of the past wasn't going to
color her judgment. Nor was she going to allow her
own lingering memories to influence her. She'd worked
too hard to overcome all that.

Jeff didn't actually look that much like his cousin, she
reasoned, getting out of the car. Arlie's hair had been
orangy-red, and he'd been shorter and stockier. He'd
also been cocky and rebellious—which didn't seem to
be the case with Jeff.

She started toward the house, then stopped when she
noticed that the big stable door was ajar. Hadn't she
closed it shortly before leaving for the hospital?
Frowning, she went to investigate.

Without bothering to open the door farther, she
slipped inside, squinting to see in the gloom. She'd
taken a few steps down the center aisle when a shadowy figure moved at the far end of the building, near
the stall where her father stored his honey wine. Her
pulse jumping, she took another step, then waited,
poised to run if she saw any sign of threat. But the fig-

ure merely froze and then she heard a frightened whisper. "*Mon Dieu!* Serena? No, it cannot be."

Even though she hadn't heard it in twelve years, Liana recognized Sybille Valentin's voice instantly. "It's Liana," she said, a token of the old resentment sweeping through her. Jeff had claimed that Sybille no longer held the Castillos responsible for her son's death. Which was big of her, Liana thought wryly, considering Rennie had been the one drinking and driving. "What are you doing here?"

"Liana!" Sybille hurried forward. "You gave me such a fright. You've changed so much—in this bad light I thought for a moment that I was seeing your sister's ghost." She halted in front of Liana and threw her hands out dramatically. "I came to welcome you back and to see how your poor father was doing. When no one answered at the house, I decided to check out here."

"I was visiting my father at the hospital," Liana explained, noting how little the woman had changed. She wore her hair in the same classic bob, simple yet chic. Even though her face bore signs of her turbulent past, she still looked far younger than her age. A straight skirt and tailored blouse set off her trim figure, making her appear closer to forty than fifty.

"How is your father?" Sybille inquired. "When I heard about his accident, I thought, 'What terrible luck after all the unhappiness he's known.'" She shook her head reproachfully. "Too much unhappiness. But he brings it on himself because he refuses to forget the past, as I have." Uncertainty tightened her expression suddenly. "And what of you, Liana? Have you forgotten? Or do you carry the same grudge as your father?"

No, not the same grudge, Liana thought, consciously resisting the bitterness that threatened to overwhelm her. Although she doubted she'd ever be able to completely forget the terrible night of the accident or Sybille's accusations afterward, she'd learned to let go of the anger and pain that had imprisoned her for so long. She wouldn't give in to that kind of emotional bondage again, even if she did find it hard to trust Sybille's bid for reconciliation.

"I think grudges are self-defeating," she said finally. "As for my father, the doctor said he's progressing."

Sybille's brow creased with worry. "But a serious break like that will probably take a long time to heal, won't it? Who's going to run this place for him?"

"I will," Liana answered firmly. "With a little help. In fact, I was going to call you about that. Jeff Moser came by yesterday and asked me to hire him. He gave your name as a reference."

Sybille's eyebrows rose a little, but she nodded quickly. "Jeff's a good worker, unlike some of his relatives."

"That's what they said when I called the garage he worked at." Liana hesitated, reluctant to offer hospitality, yet knowing she should. "Would you like a cup of coffee or something?"

Sybille glanced at her wristwatch. "No, I have to get back to the winery. The girl I left in charge of the tasting room has to leave soon for her other job."

As they walked out into the late-afternoon sunshine, Sybille shook her head again. "I can't get over how much you've changed. Someone told me you had married. Is that true?"

Liana felt a tug of wariness, but she replied, "I was married. My husband died two years ago."

"How sad!" Sybille clucked her tongue and sighed. "Still, I think you're better off than Max. I don't think he'll ever settle down with one woman. He came close one time with a girl in France, but she backed out of marrying him at the last minute. She told him she couldn't stand the competition."

Intrigued in spite of herself, Liana asked, "You mean he was seeing other women at the time?"

Sybille shrugged. "Who knows? He's always attracted more females than any man deserved. But he's like the bumblebee—he samples one flower, then flies away to the next."

Sampling, Liana thought irritably. Was that what he'd been doing several days ago when he kissed her? Not that she really cared. Since then, she'd managed to convince herself that her response to him had been based on a memory, not on any current emotion. A good thing, too, considering his reputation.

"I must go," Sybille announced briskly. "But I hope you'll let me know if there's anything I can do."

Liana couldn't imagine asking her for help of any kind, but good manners compelled her to respond. "Thanks. I appreciate that. But I think I'll manage. Especially if Jeff can get my father's truck running." Then, because she suspected Max would get a full recap of the conversation, she added, "I'm going to clean the place up a bit and start advertising in the local papers for horses to board. With all the new upscale housing developments around here, I figure there must be a lot of people who can afford horses."

Sybille's eyes narrowed a bit. "Max told me you intend to help your father buy out his lease. Do you think that's wise, considering his health problems? Or were you planning to move here permanently to help him keep the place running?"

The idea stopped Liana cold. She'd been so involved in the overwhelming problems of enabling her father to keep the ranch, she hadn't given any thought to how he would carry on if she succeeded. For now she had to focus on pulling him out of his financial trouble first. "I'm not staying permanently," she asserted. "My home is in Oregon. If my father stays here, I'll find someone to help him." She hadn't allowed herself to think about what would happen if he lost the ranch. Not yet.

"Well, I wish you luck," Sybille replied, looking around at the obvious signs of neglect.

Liana couldn't resist asking, "Why would you do that? We both know that Max wants this land for the winery."

Sybille looked offended. "I only meant to be kind. Although, I think you're wasting your time trying to save this place. In my opinion, your father would be much better off living with you in Oregon."

"This is his home, and I'm going to do everything in my power to help him keep it."

A shadow of a frown swept over Sybille's brow, but after a moment she smiled placatingly. "I'm sure you will." She consulted her watch again and made a soft sound of dismay. "I'd better leave, or I'll make Anna late. Tell your father I hope he has a speedy recovery." Without further comment she turned and strode off toward the pasture that separated Valentin and Castillo land.

THAT EVENING, WHEN Liana related the conversation to her father, he snorted derisively. "'Speedy recovery'? Hah! More likely she's hoping gangrene will set in and kill me."

Seeing that the topic was upsetting him, Liana quickly changed the subject. "I've been making a little progress with Sonny. He actually condescended to take a lump of sugar from me yesterday. I may try grooming him next, if he'll let me."

Her father scowled. "You be careful around him, honey. He can be real mean when he wants to." He smacked the mattress in frustration. "Damn, you shouldn't have to be taking care of him at all. I never intended for you to come back here to be a ranch hand. I wanted you to help me figure out a way to buy out the lease. That and . . ." Unexpectedly, his voice thickened with another emotion. "I just wanted to have you around awhile for company. With things as tight as they've been lately, I haven't been able to get away to visit you in Oregon as much as I'd like."

Tears burned in Liana's eyes as the import of his confession struck home. He'd been lonely. Her strong,

fiercely independent father—the man who'd assured
her time after time that he enjoyed living alone—had
actually been lonely. "Oh Dad, I'm so sorry. I should
have seen that and come back sooner," she said, clasp-
ing his callused hand. "But I got so wrapped up in my
own life, especially after John died, that I—"

"Don't blame yourself," he broke in. His jaw tightened stubbornly. "I didn't want you worrying about
me. Things weren't all that bad up until the past few
years. If anyone should feel guilty, it's me. I shouldn't
have dragged you into this mess between me and Valentin. I guess I wasn't thinking clearly." He shook his
head. "Since I've been in here, I've had a lot of time to
think, and I'm beginning to see how hopeless the situation is. Maybe I should just give up now and let you
get back to your home in Oregon."

The heavy undertone of defeat in his voice disturbed
Liana. "But what would you do without the ranch?
Would you be willing to move to Oregon? You know
you're welcome."

His grizzled head moved from side to side on the pil-
low. "I couldn't live that far away from your mother
and sister. I still visit their graves from time to time."

Liana had to hide her astonishment. She'd only been
eight years old when her mother had died, but she could
still remember how stoic he'd been in his grief. And he
hadn't been given to sentimental displays afterward. At
Serena's funeral, he'd been dry-eyed and grim. Hearing him admit his feelings now, made her even more
aware of how vulnerable he'd become.

She squeezed his hand reassuringly. "If you don't want to leave, you shouldn't have to. And don't give up on the ranch yet. I have a few ideas we can try. You just concentrate on healing, and I'll handle everything else."

Her father grimaced. "There's another thing. I don't like the idea of you living alone while I'm stuck in here. Especially with a man like Valentin around. He might try anything, as bad as he wants my land."

"Quit worrying about me," she ordered with a smile. "I've dealt with a few cutthroat businessmen in my career. I can handle Max." *As long as he doesn't kiss you,* an inner voice added.

TWO DAYS LATER, MAX was the furthest thing from Liana's mind as she struggled to get Sonny out of his stall. She'd managed to snap a lead on his halter, but the fractious stallion snorted and whinnied, refusing to be led outside.

"Need some help?" Max's voice sounded unexpectedly behind her, and she whirled around.

"Good grief! What are you doing here?" she demanded, her heart pounding. Sonny jerked on the lead and she almost dropped it. "You nearly scared me to death."

He grinned an apology. "Sorry. I tried the house first, then I heard the horse carrying on, so I came out to see if you were okay."

Caught off guard, she felt the force of his attractiveness buffet her like a huge wave. How could a man look so spectacular in a pair of faded jeans and a blue chambray shirt? "I'm just fine," she said, gritting her teeth against the surge of her pulse. With a backward stab of her thumb she indicated Sonny, who had ceased his protests and was now whickering a soft greeting to Max. "He's the one with the problem. I need to get him outside so I can clean his stall and groom him, but he's acting as if I'm leading him off to the glue factory." She gave the horse a disparaging look. "Not a bad idea, actually."

Chuckling, Max tugged the leather lead out of her hand before she could think to stop him. "Here, allow me." He made a soft clucking sound with his tongue and calmly started toward the barn door. To Liana's disgust, the stallion hesitated only a second before docilely following. "Where do you want him tied?" Max inquired over his shoulder.

Liana blew out an exasperated breath. "Out in the front paddock—same place he was the day he tried to do away with my father." After scooping up the bucket containing the grooming implements, she tagged after them. When Max had crosstied Sonny to the posts in the middle of the paddock, she said, "Thanks, but I could've managed. After all, I was raised around horses."

Max didn't look convinced. "Uh-huh. Hand me the currycomb and brush, will you?"

"I can take over from here." Ignoring his outstretched hand, she started toward the horse, but Sonny snorted and shied sideways. "Easy, boy," she crooned— to no avail.

"Ready to let me try?" Max inquired.

Irked, she turned and dropped the bucket at his feet. "Fine, go for it. But I think you should know my father's insurance probably won't cover your medical bills if the brute decides to stomp on you."

"He won't do that," Max replied in a low, soothing voice, one hand already gliding over the horse's dark flank. "Will you, boy?" Sonny let out a low contented sound and stood stock-still as Max went to work.

Feeling as if she'd just been judged and found wanting, Liana crossed her arms over her chest and quipped, "Very impressive. I thought your charm only worked on female homo sapiens."

Max sent her a sharp glance, but continued speaking in the same deep seductive tone as he stroked the brush over Sonny's back. "Obviously you've forgotten—your dad taught me how to ride and take care of horses."

She hadn't forgotten. From the time Max was eleven or twelve, he'd hung around the ranch every minute he could spare from his chores at home. Back then, the difference between his and Liana's ages had seemed like light-years. He'd barely acknowledged her existence, and she'd revered the very ground he walked on. At first it had been simple hero worship—uncomplicated admiration for an older boy who seemed able to do anything. But then, almost overnight, it had blossomed into the painful ecstasy of unrequited love.

Watching now, as he tugged the brush through the tangles in Sonny's luxuriant mane, she remembered vividly several occasions when she'd lain hidden in the hayloft, mesmerized by the athletic grace of his body as he groomed one of her father's horses. How she had tingled and glowed with nascent, half-formed yearnings! How her young heart had pounded—

Just as it was pounding now, she realized with alarm. Yet she couldn't tear her gaze away from the entrancing sight he made, his shining ebony hair just brushing the collar of his shirt in back, his powerful shoulders straining the pale blue fabric as he worked. And then there was the captivating fit of his jeans . . . .

He turned and caught her staring, and she felt the heat of a blush touch her cheekbones.

"Why are you looking at me like that?" he asked, pausing with one arm propped on Sonny's withers.

Liana silently chastised herself. With his experience, he probably could read her like a book. "L-Like what?" she stammered.

He smiled slightly and began to walk toward her. "You're giving me those Bambi eyes again," he murmured. "You had the same look when I kissed you the other day."

"Th-that was shock and outrage," she replied, automatically backing away from his slow advance.

"Outrage?" He shook his head. "I don't think so. Although I can believe the shock part. I was a little stunned, myself. You pack quite a wallop, sweetheart." He looked right at her mouth as he spoke, and her lips began to tingle under the warmth of his gaze. "In fact, I'd like to kiss you again, just to see if it was a fluke."

He'd felt it too? she wondered. She was having enough trouble handling her own wayward responses at the moment; she didn't need the added pressure of his sensual curiosity. "You can't kiss me," she said inanely. Her shoulder grazed the gatepost as she backed out of the paddock.

"Why not?" he retorted, coming after her just fast enough to maintain a distance of about three feet between them.

"Because I don't want you to."

"Really? That's not what your eyes are saying to me." He graced her with one of his devastating smiles.

Liana felt a surge of something wild and scary within her, and she had to look away from him. "You—You're misreading the situation."

"Am I? Then why don't you stop running away from me and convince me I'm wrong?" He stopped. "Come on, Liana. Look right into my eyes and tell me you didn't feel anything. Tell me you don't remember the first time we kissed, years ago. Was it as powerful for you as it was for me that time?"

A spark of anger flared to life inside her, overriding her trepidation. "How dare you ask that?" she challenged, nearly toppling over backward when her foot bumped into a bucket of water she'd left out earlier. "That kiss didn't have any effect on you. You shoved me away, remember?" She stopped and propped her hands on her hips. "And then you acted as if I'd ceased to exist."

Max looked confounded. "What did you expect me to do? You were just a kid."

"I was fourteen," she shot back, her temper threatening to boil over.

"You were also suffering from a monumental case of puppy love." He shook his head in bemusement. "What amazes me is that the incident still upsets you this much. It almost sounds as if you never got over that crush."

"Of all the conceited. . ." Words failed her as the burning force of her indignation wiped out years of self-control. The fact that there might have been a kernel of truth in his claim only made her more angry. Furious, she looked about for some means of retaliation. Like a gift from heaven, the water bucket stood waiting at her feet. Without a second thought, she picked it up and heaved the contents at him, soaking him from head to toe.

Stunned silence reigned as the possible consequences of her action dawned on her. For a moment, Max just looked at her as rivulets of water streamed down his face. Then his expression darkened and he started toward her. Startled, Liana dropped the bucket and made a dash for the stable, intending to blockade herself in the tack room. Unfortunately, Max was too fast for her. She'd only reached the first stall inside when his strong arms wrapped around her from behind and they toppled onto a pile of hay.

Up to that point, she'd felt panicky, but when Max neatly pinned her beneath him, her wrists imprisoned in his hands, sheer terror took over—a terror rooted in the memory of another time she'd been held like that, trapped beneath the conquering weight of a male body. She felt hysteria rise within her and she tried to scream. Only a choked sound came out as she thrashed about wildly.

Dimly she was aware of Max's voice saying, "Liana, for God's sake . . ." as he tried to hold her down. But then, with a suddenness that left her momentarily stunned, his weight left her and she was free to roll to her side in a tight ball of misery.

"Liana, honey, I'm sorry. I never intended to upset you like this."

She flinched at the touch of his hand on her shoulder, but he kept it there, stroking her gently. At first she couldn't stop the shudders that racked her body, but slowly she felt herself begin to calm. Before long, the shaking subsided as Max's deep voice reached out to her in a soothing litany.

"I'd never hurt you," he said softly. "You must know that. I admit I lost my head for a second when you doused me, but I never intended to do anything but kiss you. Can't you believe that?"

Could she? Liana wondered, as his warm hand sought to ease the tension from her shoulders. Now that she could view things from a calmer perspective, she had to admit that the worst of her panic had been based on memories of the boy who'd used his superior size to assault her. Max had never done anything to harm her physically. She nodded her assent, not quite able to speak just yet.

"Good," he said, sounding enormously relieved. "Now, can you tell me why you were so frightened?"

Tell him about Arlie? No, she couldn't do that. Not even John had known the full story. She shook her head and sighed convulsively.

"All right, then, would you mind if I just put my arm around you for a while? Because it's killing me to see you huddled up like that."

Surprised at the hint of desperation she detected in his voice, she couldn't bring herself to refuse. "I—I guess it's okay," she whispered, willing herself not to shift away as he slid down behind her on the rustling hay and gently placed one arm around her waist. She could feel his body curved around hers, and even though his arm was the only part touching her, the warmth of him reached out to her like a full-length embrace.

After a moment he said, "Are you sure you won't tell me why you were so terrified? I've never done anything to make you think I'd harm you, have I?"

Unable to lie, she shook her head. "No, it wasn't you. I . . . I just don't want to talk about it."

"Then would you mind letting me tell my side of what happened that first time we kissed? Right before I was treated to the impromptu shower, you accused me of not feeling anything. You're wrong. On the contrary, I felt too much."

She glanced over her shoulder, not bothering to hide her disbelief.

Max clasped her shoulder, compelling her to keep looking at him. "It's the truth. There I was, a cool guy of nineteen, who thought he knew just about everything about women. Then this fourteen-year-old—a girl I'd known since she was in pigtails—kisses me and I nearly lose it."

She inhaled sharply. Surely he didn't mean... "What are you saying?" she asked breathlessly.

"I mean I got hot—aroused—whatever you want to call it. I wanted you, sweetheart. Against all reason and conscience, I wanted to make love to you. You came to me offering comfort, and I wanted to lay you down on the grass and bury myself in your sweet innocent body. *That's* why I pushed you away and avoided you like the plague from then on. Based on how I felt after just one kiss, I didn't trust myself around you."

He tugged harder on her shoulder, urging her over onto her back. "And," he continued, bringing his face dangerously close to hers. "Based on what I felt the other day in my storage room, your effect on me hasn't weakened at all over the years."

"Max," she began, intending to tell him to back off. But the words floated away like dust motes in a sunbeam as she stared into the brilliant blue of his eyes.

His hand moved from her shoulder, and she felt his fingertips ride up the sensitive curve of her neck and over the hollow of her cheek. Slowly he traced the arch of her eyebrow and the straight line of her nose. Then his forefinger grazed her lips, and she felt as if she'd been kissed by fire.

"You are so incredibly beautiful," he said slowly, his voice resonating with sensual intent. "I want to kiss you again. Would you object to that?"

At the moment she couldn't think why. She tried to summon her wits, but the best she could come up with was a breathless, "You shouldn't."

"Why not?" His fingertip trailed over her mouth again, sensitizing it until she thought she'd go mad. "You're not a kid anymore."

Her heart was pounding again, but it wasn't from fear this time. A dizzying anticipation filled her. "Max..." she whispered. But her protest came out sounding like a plea.

"Yes," he murmured, slowly moving closer until their mouths touched. The sweetness of it made her gasp, and she reached, without thinking, to clasp his head... to prolong the heavenly contact. His hair felt like silk beneath her fingers, and at her touch his mouth settled more firmly over hers. With an electrifying flick of his tongue, he parted her lips.

For Liana the entire universe seemed to condense to the warm pressure of Max's mouth. Nothing else mattered, nothing else existed. She only wanted more. When his tongue claimed the soft interior of her mouth, she surrendered to it eagerly. When he pulled back a bit, teasing her with just the faintest brush of his damp mouth against hers, she uttered a moan of impatience and lifted her lips to his in silent demand.

A low growl of need rumbled in his chest as he took what she offered. This time his tongue plunged deep and the force of his conquest took her breath away. Liana felt as if she were on a carousel, spinning around and around, totally out of control.

She heard Max groan and whisper, "Liana." He moved closer, his fingers gently gripping her chin. But when she felt the weight of his chest settling against her breasts, the merry-go-round began to grind to a halt.

Instinctively her hands slid down to his shoulders, bracing against the pressure. Almost at once she felt his reaction. His muscles tensed and flexed beneath her fingers as he sensed her resistance and eased back. Then he tore his mouth away from hers, breathing like a man who'd just run a marathon.

She turned her head to the side, dismayed to realize she was panting, also. Her pulse surged through her body like a hot tide, stirring wild and alien sensations. She felt adrift, out of control, and she didn't like it.

Sensual urgency vibrated in Max's voice when he spoke. "Liana.... Damn, that was unbelievable." But when he touched her cheek, trying to make her look at him, she kept her face averted. "What happened?" he inquired. "A few seconds ago, you seemed to be enjoying it as much as I. What went wrong?"

She shook her head and tried to turn away, but he stayed her with a hand on her shoulder. "Come on, you at least owe me an explanation."

She forcibly brought her breathing under control and faced him. "All right, I'll be frank. I don't like all that heavy-breathing stuff. It... It disgusts me." Even to her it sounded like a lie, so she wasn't surprised when Max refused to believe her.

"I'm not buying that. Not after the way you just kissed me. You were right with me until I tried to get closer." He paused thoughtfully. "That's the key, isn't it? You didn't back off until I pressed against you. And you freaked out when I pinned you down a while ago. Why, Liana?"

Apprehension suddenly choked her. She didn't want to talk about this. Especially not now, not with him. "That's not your business," she said tightly.

"I think it is, after that last kiss. Was it the guy you married?" His expression darkened. "Did he mistreat you?"

If she hadn't been so upset, she might have laughed. John had been the kindest, gentlest man she'd ever known. His love for her had been steadfast and unqualified, in spite of her initial resistance to the idea of marriage. Patiently, he'd worn down her resistance, convincing her that the affection she felt for him could grow into love in time. Even when she'd been unable to respond fully to his lovemaking, he'd never complained.

"No, it wasn't my husband," she replied, shrugging away from the hand that held her shoulder. When he let her go, she scrambled to her feet and retreated to the doorway of the stall. "Don't bother asking me any more questions, because I won't answer them." Fortified by the advantage of standing while he remained sprawled on the hay, she added, "I think you'd better leave now."

Max frowned. "No. Not until I finish what I started." He got up slowly, brushing the hay from his jeans and shirt.

When he started toward her, she took several hasty steps backward. "I thought I made myself clear. I'm not interested in your—your attentions," she snapped.

He gave her a wry look. "You may not be, but I'll bet Sonny is. I'll finish grooming him before I go."

"You don't need to do that," she said, pride making her stand her ground as he stopped in front of her. "I can manage."

His brows lowered reprovingly. "Look at it this way. At the moment, I could use the exercise to work off some of the frustration I'm feeling—sexual and otherwise." He ran his hands down the side seams of his jeans, subtly adjusting the fit.

Without thinking, Liana glanced down and saw the unmistakable bulge beneath his fly. Embarrassed, she quickly looked away, but he'd already noticed. Catching her chin in his palm, he brought his face close to hers and drawled, "I still want you, Liana. So don't think that I'm giving up on this other business between us. I'm going to discover your secret, and then I'm going to help you overcome it."

The sheer audacity of his claim provoked her into asking, "Is that a service you provide for all of your conquests?"

His mouth tightened for a moment, then he smiled wickedly. "Only for the ones who have Bambi eyes."

Before she could think of a cutting retort, he turned and strode out of the stable. When he returned a while later, leading Sonny and the horse she'd ridden, she made a point of not looking up from the bridle she'd been cleaning.

But after securing the two horses in their respective stalls, Max came to stand before her. "Ignoring me isn't going to change anything," he said with a trace of exasperation in his voice.

Resolutely, she kept her eyes down. "Goodbye, Max."

"No, not good-bye." He reached to cup her chin, compelling her to look at him. "Until next time."

He left without another word, but as she watched him go, she could feel the force of his determination battering against the walls of her safe, controlled world.

5

BRIGHT APRIL SUNSHINE warmed Liana's back as she leaned over the dented fender of her father's truck and surveyed the greasy environs of the engine. From the other side of the vehicle, Jeff offered her an encouraging grin. "It looks worse than it actually is," he said, reaching with a wrench to loosen something. "These old trucks were built tough. I should have her running in a week, if I can find the parts."

"I hope you're right," she replied doubtfully. At the moment, the situation at Castillo's Arabians still looked pretty hopeless. There'd been a few calls in response to the advertisement she'd run in the local paper, but no one had actually shown up with a horse to be boarded. After a long telephone conversation with her stepson, Eric, she'd come to the conclusion that she couldn't pull her money out of the winery. That left the local banks, and her experience as an accountant told her they wouldn't be eager to loan money unless she could think of some way to guarantee repayment.

She rubbed her temples wearily. There was so much to be done, and so little capital to do it with. The only good news was, Max hadn't been around to bother her since that upsetting incident in the stable two days before.

"I hope you don't mind my saying this, but you look like you're working too hard." Jeff's voice snagged her attention. He was studying her from his side of the truck. "Sybille said she's worried about you."

Liana raised her eyebrows in surprise. "Sybille? When did she tell you that?"

For an instant, he looked as if he'd been caught making a gaffe, then he ducked his head over the engine and mumbled, "Oh, the other day. I was doing some stuff for her."

She couldn't see his face, but the tips of his ears were bright red, making her wonder at the cause. Had Sybille said something about her that embarrassed him? Or was he just ashamed to admit he'd been listening to gossip?

Liana decided not to distress him further by pursuing it. "Well, you can tell her that I'm in perfect health," she said.

Jeff seemed to sink lower into the depths of the engine. "Uh—yeah, if I see her again anytime soon." She didn't give the incident further thought until later that morning when Jeff's sister, Brenna, arrived to give him a ride to his other job. Brenna appeared to be several years younger than Jeff, and although she had the same pallid blue eyes and pale blond hair, her round face was open and friendly. The pickup she drove was even more dilapidated than the one her brother was trying to fix, but she was dressed neatly in a starched waitress's uniform.

Jeff had taken Max's car into town to buy truck parts, so Liana went out to greet his sister in the shade of the

oak trees. After the usual amenities, Brenna tilted her
head to one side and said forthrightly, "You're not what
I expected."

Instantly wary, Liana replied, "Oh? And what was
that?"

Brenna shrugged. "I don't know. Maybe someone a
little more sexy-flashy, you know? Instead, you look
kinda reserved and sophisticated."

Gossip again, Liana thought with a little flare of resentment. Her voice dripped with sarcasm as she retorted, "Not at all like one of those trashy Castillo girls
you heard about, right? I suppose the whole valley is
buzzing with the old gossip, now that I'm back."

Unfazed, Brenna flipped one hand dismissively.
"Nah. First of all, there aren't that many of the old gossips left. Most of the people who live here now haven't
even heard of you. The only reason I know the story is
because I overheard my mom and my aunt talking
about it one time. Mom was kinda worried because Jeff
took his cousin's death so hard."

A shadow of disquiet flitted through the recesses of
Liana's mind. "Oh? I had no idea they were close.
Wasn't—" She paused, stumbling over the name she
didn't want to remember. "Wasn't his cousin quite a bit
older?"

"Nine years. It was like hero worship on Jeff's part."

Some hero, Liana thought with an inner shudder.

"Anyway, I don't think you need to worry about the
story getting around again," Brenna added, shrugging. "It's been ancient history for a long time. Even if

it wasn't, anybody looking at you would find it hard to believe all that junk about you and your sister."

The clumsy assurance was offered with such a lack of guile, Liana couldn't help liking the girl. "Thanks for the vote of confidence."

Brenna had apparently tired of that subject, because she looked around and said, "I hear you're fixing the place up. You going to breed Arabians, like before?"

Liana had to laugh. "Not until I find a way to change the personality of my father's stallion. Right now I'm looking for people who want to board their horses. We've got a few boarders here now, but there's room for a lot more."

"There're already a couple of boarding stables in the valley. But with all the new housing, you might be able to pull in a fair amount of business," Brenna said. "I'll keep my ears open at work—a lot of the locals eat there. If I hear of anyone looking to board a horse, I'll send them your way."

Warmed by the gesture, Liana smiled. "I'd appreciate that."

"Speaking of locals . . ." Brenna leaned closer, a just-between-us look on her plain face. "Have you run into *him* yet?" She jerked her thumb in the direction of the Valentin property.

In more ways than one, Liana reflected, but she wasn't going to admit it. "Who?" she asked, playing dumb.

Brenna rolled her eyes. "You know, Max Valentin, the heartbreaker."

"Good grief, do people actually call him that?"

A sly smile curved the girl's mouth. "A certain segment of the female population has reason to. I suspect a good portion of the single ladies in this valley have had a thing for him at one time or another. Some of the married ones, too."

Liana realized she shouldn't encourage Brenna's gossiping, but she had to ask, "How many of their hearts do you suppose he's broken?"

Brenna chuckled. "More than his fair share. He's had that sort of Continental air about him ever since his stay in France. I can tell you, the women really flocked around him when he came back to take over the winery."

Something tightened in Liana's chest, but she managed a mocking smile. "Sounds like a mob scene to me. I can't believe the man is worth all that."

"Maybe. But I talked to a woman who kissed him once, and she said it was sheer heaven."

Like a hot gust of desert air, the memory of Max's kiss swept over Liana's senses. Even as the thought of him kissing another woman repelled her, the memory of how his mouth had felt on hers made her quiver inside. "He must need Herculean strength, keeping all of his admirers happy."

"Oh, he doesn't even try to do that." Brenna made a face. "That's how he got the heartbreaker nickname. Most of us just admire him from afar. Those who have gotten close to him, generally regret it, because he never gets as heavily involved as they do."

"Just strings them along, huh?" Liana inquired, feeling sick. The afternoon heat suddenly felt oppressive, even in the shade.

"Not really. As I understand it, he's real up-front about his feelings from the start. And he has this policy of not going out with more than one at a time."

Liana knew she should let the subject die there, but a burning need to know compelled her to ask, "Who's the current lucky lady?"

Squinting thoughtfully, Brenna replied, "Now that you ask, I'm not real sure. He's sorta dropped out of the social scene around here lately." She grinned self-consciously. "Not that I circulate in that crowd. But I have a friend who's going out with a guy who does." Her head jerked guiltily at the sound of an approaching car. "Oops. I'll bet that's Jeff. Do me a favor, don't let on that I told you all that stuff about Max. My brother thinks I talk too much."

Liana nodded and turned to greet Jeff with a wave.

BY EARLY EVENING the temperature had cooled considerably, thanks to the fresh ocean breeze that wafted though Rainbow Gap, a break in the mountains embracing the western side of the valley. But Liana's mind still simmered with the memory of Brenna's words.

"He's a lot like you," she muttered to Sonny as she shooed him inside from the small paddock adjoining his stall. "No emotional involvement, just the basic biological functions. How could I have been so gullible, allowing him to kiss me like that?" She slammed the Dutch door, securing the horse in his stall for the night.

"That guy still giving you trouble?" Max's voice came unexpectedly from the shadows on the east side of the barn.

Liana nearly jumped out of her skin. "What are you doing here?"

Max glanced at her quizzically. "I just happened to be in the neighborhood. How are you and Mr. Macho doing?"

Liana clenched her jaw. "We're wonderful. He's practically eating out of my hand," she replied. Just the sight of Max standing there, so incredibly handsome and at ease with his charm, made her remember all the things Brenna had said.

"Eating out of your hand, hmm?" he responded, looking utterly unconvinced. "Since all of your fingers seem to be intact, would you mind telling me which one of us is responsible for your current mood?"

"I just don't like unexpected company," she said, quickly climbing over the paddock fence. As she came down on the other side, Max's large hands clasped her hips from behind, steadying her, and she felt as if she'd been zapped with electricity. "I can manage," she snapped, then promptly lost her footing in her haste to be free of his touch.

He caught her with one arm around her waist, and for an endless moment she felt the vital warmth of his body down the length of her back. Then he gently lowered her until her feet touched the ground.

Her senses in an uproar, Liana wrenched away from his grip and whirled to face him. "That wouldn't have happened if you hadn't grabbed me. Would you, please, just leave me alone?"

Max's mouth quirked in dry amusement. "Easier said than done, sweetheart. Especially considering the way you kiss."

She flushed. "Don't bring that up again. And don't call me sweetheart. I'm not a part of your extensive harem."

"So you're back to that again." His expression clouded. "Who's been feeding you gossip now?"

"It's pretty hard to avoid the subject around here, given your reputation." She turned and started walking toward the house.

Undaunted, he accompanied her, easily matching her stride. "What have I been accused of this time?"

"Nothing more than your usual bedroom Olympics. From what I've heard, if they ever open an event in your area of expertise, you're a sure bet for a gold medal." She knew she was provoking him, but anger seemed to be the only weapon at her disposal. If she made him mad enough, he might go away.

His low growl told her she'd succeeded in the first part of her plan, but his reaction wasn't what she'd hoped for. Instead, he grabbed her arm and forced her to stop and face him. His azure eyes blazed with outrage. "You make me sound like some kind of stallion. Is that how you picture me, indiscriminately servicing the female population? Because I have news for you, love. I gave up promiscuity long ago. With my work schedule lately, I haven't even had time for more than an occasional date. There've been women in my life, but not the multitudes you're suggesting."

He looked so indignant, she began to wonder if she'd judged him unfairly, but she couldn't allow herself to back down. "How reassuring. Why don't you go bother one of them, instead of me?"

She started toward the house again, but he caught her by the shoulders. "Because I can't remember one of them driving me wild with a single kiss, like you do. I get turned on just thinking about you." The fire in his eyes began to smolder sensually, and she felt an unnerving glow of response deep inside her.

"I told you, I'm not interested," she said, with a little less certainty.

"No. What you are is scared. I still want to know why. You said it wasn't your late husband. Was it a boyfriend that hurt you? Did some guy force himself on you?"

She looked away, the ancient turmoil stirring within her like a brewing storm. She didn't want to talk about it, and least of all with him.

"That's it, isn't it?" His voice softened. "When did it happen?" He gave her shoulders a gentle squeeze. "Come on, Liana, talk to me. Was it someone you knew?"

Her agitation swelled to the breaking point. No, she hadn't known him, not until it was too late.

Max's hands tightened insistently. "I'm not going to give up until you tell me."

Suddenly the storm inside her broke, unleashing a torrent of emotions she'd thought long vanquished.

"You Valentin men are all alike, pushing and pushing . . . never giving up until you get your way. Rennie was even worse. He kept taunting me, calling me a tomboy, saying I couldn't get a guy if I tried." Furious, she shoved at the hands that held her shoulders.

Looking completely dumbfounded, Max released her. "Rennie? What does he have to do with this?" A sick horror swept over his face. "Oh, damn. Was he the one?"

Liana turned on him, all reticence momentarily forgotten. "No, but he might as well have been. He was the one who talked me into going out with Arlie Moser, and then left me alone with the guy, while he and my sister took a little 'stroll' in the moonlight. He actually laughed when they came back and found out what had happened." Even now, she could remember Rennie's sneering face and Serena's fury.

"Arlie Moser," Max repeated, his voice heavy. "He was the other one who died the night of the crash, wasn't he?"

"Yes. The night your stepbrother killed my sister." Without warning, the old grief hit her, its pain still potent after all these years. Serena. Sweet, lovely Serena. Cut off in the first bloom of life, just because she fell in love with the wrong boy. Suddenly anguish engulfed her and she was seized by a need to escape.

She turned and sprinted for the house, her throat tight with unshed tears. *Let them come*—that's what Dr. Cramer had said when the lingering effects of her ordeal had imprisoned her voice. *When the tears start, you'll begin to heal.*

And she *had* learned to cry eventually, but she needed privacy to do it. She entered the kitchen at a run, slamming the door behind her, but she couldn't manage the lock before Max shoved it open again. *Get out*, her mind screamed, but the words wouldn't come. She moved to put the breakfast table between them, averting her face so he wouldn't see the wet streaks beneath her eyes.

"Liana, I want to help," he said gently.

More tears spilled over her cheeks and she dashed at them with a trembling hand. She turned to press her head against the wall, wanting to hide her grief.

She heard his footsteps approaching and a moment later his warm hands wrapped around her waist. "Liana," he said with heartbreaking tenderness. "Let me hold you. I feel your pain."

To her surprise, his embrace seemed to vanquish some of her pain and the constriction in her throat began to ease. Still, a part of her couldn't give in to the comfort he offered . She quickly pushed his hands away, and stepped toward the living room, inhaling a deep breath. "I don't need your help," she managed in a quavery whisper. "I've had counseling."

"Maybe. But based on what I've seen, you're still hung up on what happened that night."

She sent him a sharp glance over her shoulder. "Even if I am, I don't see how it concerns you."

"Because I care about what happened . . . and about you."

His response caused a flutter in her chest, and she replied sarcastically to counter it. "Interesting words, especially coming from the man who's trying to take my father's land away from him."

He gently squeezed her shoulder. "That has nothing to do with what's happening between us, and you know it. The real issue here is your aversion to sex."

Shocked, she spun around to face him. "That's ridiculous. I was happily married for two years."

Max's expression tightened. "So, you're telling me that you and your husband had a full sexual relationship?"

"Absolutely," she shot back. But she knew it was a lie. She'd tolerated John's lovemaking, but it had never been more than accommodation on her part.

For a moment, Max seemed taken aback, but then he tried again. "You never had any reservations when he made love to you? You never pushed him away?"

"I don't have to answer that." She tried to glare at him but couldn't meet the intensity of his gaze. John had known how she felt, and he'd always been terribly careful.

"I'm just trying to determine whether or not this happy marriage of yours included any passion. Because you're loaded with it, honey. Yet, the other day when I kissed you, you claimed to be disgusted by the 'heavy-breathing stuff.' Did you tell your husband that, too?"

Once again he'd homed in on the truth. Liana felt as if he'd probed her innermost secrets, leaving her exposed and vulnerable. "Damn you," she whispered, turning away to seek the dimly lit security of the living room. She curled herself in a corner of the old chintz-covered sofa, wanting only to escape the knowing look in his eyes. Too soon Max's weight tilted the cushion beneath her, and although he didn't attempt to touch her, his presence was tangible.

"Liana, listen to me," he said with quiet intensity. "I'm not doing this to hurt you. That's the last thing I want."

She kept her face pressed into the worn armrest. "What *do* you want, then?" Her control was slipping again, as it seemed to do so often when he was near.

"I want to know about the night that did this to you. I've heard all of the rumors. Now I need to hear the truth, so I can help you overcome your fear."

"I don't think anyone can do that," she replied. But the earnestness she heard in his voice almost made her wish he could.

"Try me," he urged.

She felt his hands come down on her shoulders. He began a gentle massage, working against her resistance. "I wouldn't know where to begin."

"Anywhere that feels right to you. You said that Rennie and Serena went off and left you alone with Arlie. Where were you?"

She considered not answering him, but the touch of his hands was so comforting, the tone of his voice so kind and compelling, all her reasons for not telling him seemed to fade into insignificance.

"We were up near Mount Palomar," she began hesitantly. "We'd been to a movie, and then Rennie drove there to park and drink beer. I objected, but he and Arlie just laughed and called me a baby. Serena kept promising me it'd only be for a little while." Max's fingers continued their motion, working against the tightness in her neck. Warmth began to radiate through her body.

"There wasn't anyone else around to help you that night?"

"No. I screamed a couple of times before . . . before he got his hand over my mouth, but it didn't do any good." She paused, surprised at how easily that had come out, then added, "Struggling didn't help, either. He just used his weight to hold me down on the car seat."

Max uttered a low growl of fury. "He must have hurt you a lot. I wish there were some way I could make him pay for that. Rennie, too."

The fierce vengefulness in his voice reassured her so much, she went on. "It wasn't just what he did. He said . . . terrible things to me." Even now the memory could still make her shiver. Max must have felt it, because he pulled her back against his chest, lightly wrapping his arms around her waist. They sat staring straight ahead at the brick fireplace, with its assortment of knickknacks and old family portraits cluttering the mantel.

Max didn't speak but she could sense his concern compelling her to go on.

"He just kept telling me it was my fault. That I'd led him on. That he knew I was as . . . horny as he was. Then he started talking about all kinds of disgusting things that he was going to do to me. He kept that up even after he was . . . finished. I tried to get out of the car, but he wouldn't let me. By the time Rennie and Serena got back, I was crying so hysterically I could hardly speak."

"I'm not surprised. Liana, you weren't responsible, no matter what that creep told you. Rape is an act of aggression. It has nothing to do with passion."

"I . . . I know that. I heard it enough times from Dr. Cramer."

"Good." Max appeared to think for a minute, then said, "You told me Rennie laughed when he found out what happened. What did Serena do?"

Liana bit her lip and frowned. "She was furious. She almost attacked Arlie, but Rennie grabbed her and threw her in the backseat with me. She started screaming at Rennie, insisting that he take us home immediately. Both of the guys had been drinking most of the evening, and when Rennie started driving back down the mountain, he began acting crazy and showing off."

She pressed a hand to her forehead. This was where the story always dimmed, where the memories dissolved into a black mist. "I—I don't remember much after that. The official report said that Rennie missed a curve and we went over the edge and down about two hundred feet before we hit a tree. They tell me I pulled my sister from the wreckage just before the gas tank exploded, but it didn't make any difference. She was already dead." Fighting another wave of sadness, Liana tipped her head back and found it cushioned by Max's broad shoulder.

"What a hellish night," he murmured with quiet intensity. "No wonder you couldn't speak afterward."

She sighed as she felt his fingertips trace the sensitive line of her throat. "It got worse. Somehow the news leaked out that Serena was pregnant when she died. The gossips had a field day with that. By association, I was judged and found guilty, too, even though I'd never—"

"You were a virgin," he supplied, when she faltered. "I figured that." He sighed heavily. "What a damnable initiation to sex. It's no wonder you're put off by heavy breathing." His fingers stroked the length of her throat again. "You don't have to answer this if you don't want to, but I'm wondering how your husband handled all this."

Normally, she would have balked at the intimacy of his question, but after all she'd told him so far, it seemed a minor step to go on. "He didn't know all of it, but he knew enough. And he never asked for more than I could give."

Max turned his head, angling it down so he could gaze into her eyes questioningly. Even in the half-light the intense blue of his eyes sent a power surge of sensation through her.

"I couldn't give him passion," she said.

"I'd like to help you change that." He shifted subtly, easing her around until her head rested on the hard curve of his biceps. A dreamy sensuality seemed to soften his face as he looked at her.

"Max, I can't," she said, as her heart began a betraying double-time beat.

"Can't what? Kiss me?" His face moved closer. "No. If you'll recall, our kissing wasn't a problem. And that's all I want from you right now." His mouth glanced across hers, so firm, yet smooth and warm. It tickled unbearably. He did it again . . . and again, until her lips burned. When she could stand no more, she lifted her mouth to take what he offered so teasingly. Incredible sweetness flooded through her—not the distressing wildness she'd expected. His lips clung to hers with exquisite tenderness, coaxing her response.

In spite of everything, she began to give in to it. She felt bereft when he pulled away after only a short time.

"Did that frighten you?" he asked a bit breathlessly.

Slowly she moved her head from side to side, her gaze never leaving his.

His smile broke over her like a summer sunrise. "Then maybe we should try it again." The smile was still there when their lips touched, and she felt it to the depths of her soul. But even though the tip of his tongue flicked out to taste her, the kiss never got out of control. And when Max broke it off, she was left wanting more.

To her disappointment, he released her and moved away. "I'd better leave before this escalates into more than you can handle." He regarded her uncertainly. "Unless you'd rather not be alone for a while. I know it was difficult for you, digging all that up."

"No, I'm fine now," she said quickly, to keep herself from begging him to stay and kiss her again. Amazingly enough, she really did feel better than before— although she didn't allow herself to decide whether talking things out or being kissed by Max was responsible. She stood, and when he followed suit, she led the way back through the kitchen and outside.

The moon hung like a luminescent ivory disk in the night sky, and the high-pitched strumming of crickets filled the air. "I want to see you again," Max said, reaching to touch her cheek.

She'd switched the porch light on before stepping outside and now, in its revealing glow, she could see the gleam of tightly restrained desire in his eyes. Even though she'd yearned for more of his kisses a few moments ago, seeing his need reawakened her reserve. "I'm awfully busy," she hedged.

"Too busy, if you ask me. You've been pushing yourself ever since you arrived here. What you need is a little R and R." He smiled engagingly. "How about going out to dinner with me tomorrow night? One of the local wineries has a great restaurant that serves gourmet food."

The offer tempted her unbearably. She *had* been working awfully hard lately, and the idea of relaxing and letting someone else provide her dinner sounded heavenly. Still, a part of her held back. "I don't think—"

"No, don't think," he interrupted gently. "Just say yes. Think of it as a business dinner, if you like. You can tell me all about your winery in Oregon." He smiled again. "I promise you won't regret it."

She wasn't sure if she could agree with that, but she relented anyway. "All right. But I can't stay out too late."

"Don't worry. You're not the only one who has to get up early." He left then, after promising to return for her the following night at six.

AS HE STRODE ACROSS the pasture that bordered his vineyards, Max was glad he'd walked over, rather than driven. He needed the fresh air and exercise to clear his head before he started planning his next move with Liana. And there *would* be a next move, he thought, climbing over the last fence and heading toward the pond. Now that he knew the story behind Liana's reticence, he intended to do everything in his power to replace those bad memories with beautiful ones. He wanted to see the fear and uncertainty in her lovely eyes turn to a mindless hunger that would match his own.

He sighed heavily and paused at the edge of the pond. The water looked invitingly cool in the moonlight. His temperature still hadn't come down from those kisses, even though he'd been careful not to overwhelm Liana with the full intensity of his desire. The effect she had on him was nothing short of incredible.

He made a quick decision and began pulling off his clothes. A little smile curved his mouth as it occurred to him how shocked she would be if she knew he was skinny-dipping in her father's pond. No, that wasn't quite right; the pond, along with all of the Castillo land, was his.

That was another problem, he thought, standing naked in the balmy night air. She was wearing herself out, trying to salvage the place. Even though that was

in direct opposition to his plans, he didn't like to think
of how she would feel if she failed.

He shook his head at the incongruity of his feelings
and waded out into the pond. The woman was going
to drive him crazy—in more ways than one! He gasped
as the chilly water embraced his overheated groin, then
gritted his teeth and dived in all the way.

BY SIX O'CLOCK THE following evening, Liana had definitely decided she couldn't possibly go to dinner with
Max. He'd told her not to think, but that was all she'd
done since he'd left last night. Every time she remembered how much she'd revealed to him, she felt a new
wave of chagrin.

As she stared at the uninspiring contents of the refrigerator, she berated herself again. Whatever had
made her spill the whole sordid story like that? Especially to Max.

The doorbell rang, and her heart thumped hard
against her chest. She'd tried to call Max during the day,
but he'd been out. She'd been forced to leave a message
on his answering machine, telling him she'd changed
her mind about dinner. But even before she opened the
front door, she knew who was waiting outside. The
sight of him standing there, the epitome of masculinity
sent her pulse racing.

His dark brown slacks and fawn sports jacket gave
him a faintly Continental look, as did the crisp white
shirt he wore open at the throat. A soft breeze blew in
the door, wafting toward her a tantalizing hint of after-
shave.

"You're giving me those Bambi eyes again," he said, reminding her that she was standing there staring at him like a fool.

"I'm just not used to seeing you dressed up, that's all," she protested hastily.

An upraised eyebrow expressed his doubt, but he didn't challenge her. Instead he sent a quick glance over her appearance. "I know Southern California has a reputation for casual dress, but I think the jeans and tank top might be a little too casual for the restaurant I have in mind."

She bit her lip nervously. Turning him down over the phone would have been so much easier. "Didn't you get my message? I'm not going."

His mouth quirked in irritation. "I not only got the message, I anticipated it. It's because of what happened yesterday, right?"

Uncomfortable, she dropped her gaze. "I never should have told you all of that."

"I disagree. You needed to talk about it, and I needed to know." He nudged her chin up with his hand. "I'd never tell anyone. You realize that, don't you?" The concern in his eyes and voice reached out to her like a warm embrace, urging her to trust him. She nodded slowly.

"Then I don't see any reason why we can't have dinner together. Unless . . ." A worried frown creased his brow. "Unless you feel I'm somehow responsible for what my stepbrother did."

The very idea distressed her. "No, that isn't it," she said quickly. "I just feel . . ."

A glimmer of understanding replaced the worry in his expression. "Vulnerable?" he supplied gently. "That scares you, doesn't it?" His thumb began to stroke the sensitive underside of her chin, sending a delicious shiver down her spine. "Don't be afraid, Liana. I'd never do anything to hurt you. Can't you believe that?"

She wasn't sure why, but at the moment she could. She nodded and his smile appeared like a bright sunbeam. "Then prove it by changing your clothes and coming with me to dinner," he urged. "I'll wait for you in the living room." Gripping her shoulders, he turned her toward the staircase and gave her a little shove. "And hurry. I've been looking forward to this all day, and I'm starving."

Still half-bedazzled by his smile, she complied. But as she quickly changed, applied a touch of makeup, and redid her hair, apprehension crept in. She checked her appearance in the mirror. The white linen chemise was simply, yet elegantly cut, perfect for almost any occasion. The scoop neckline dipped only slightly, just enough to frame her favorite turquoise-and-silver necklace. Matching earrings dangled from her ears, softening the severe effect of her hair, which she wore pulled straight back in the usual tight bun. She looked more like a woman who was going to a Sunday church service, than one who would be having dinner with the sexiest man alive.

Catching the drift of her thoughts, she let out an impatient breath. That kind of thinking could get her in deep trouble. This was going to be a simple dinner date—nothing else. If Max had other ideas, he was going to be disappointed.

He was waiting for her at the foot of the stairs, and as she descended he let out a low wolf whistle. "Incredible. And you did it in half the time most women would take."

Unsettled by his blatant admiration, she tried to deflect it with a gibe. "I suppose you're an expert on those statistics."

He gave her a mock scowl and hustled her toward the door. "Don't start that again, especially when I'm ravenous. You might not like what happens."

He'd parked his truck next to the Honda Civic and as they walked toward the vehicles, he asked, "Which coach would you prefer, Cinderella?"

A nervous laugh escaped her. "I really don't care which we take. And I think you could use a little research on your fairy tales. I don't look anything like Cinderella."

"You're right," he said, guiding her to the door of his truck, then stopping her before she could slip inside. "She couldn't have been nearly as lovely as you." His eyes took on a familiar glow as he gazed at her face. "In fact, you're so beautiful, I'd like to sweep you into my arms and kiss you until we both forget about eating dinner."

A bone-melting thrill ran through Liana, but she managed a protesting, "Max!"

He hesitated, then cleared his throat. "I know, that part comes later. For now, I'll have to content myself

with looking at you." Taking her arm, he started to help
her into the truck, but she balked.

"Wait a minute. If you're thinking that just because
I agreed to have dinner with you, I'm going to—"

"No, that isn't what I'm thinking," he cut in, placing
a finger over her lips. "Whatever happens later is up to
you. I asked you to have dinner with me because I
thought you could use a little time away from this
place." He smiled. "And because I know you won't get
bored if I go on and on about wine making."

Somewhat mollified, she allowed him to guide her
into the truck's passenger seat. But as they drove off
toward the restaurant, her mind kept dancing back to
that one word—*later*.

6

LIANA'S DOUBTS ABOUT the evening grew as Max parked in Café Chardonnay's crowded lot. There appeared to be a long line of people waiting for tables. "I hope you have a reservation," she said.

Max grinned. "Better than that. The owner is a friend." He got out and came around to open her door. "He's saving a special table for us."

The hostess welcomed Max with the kind of warmth reserved for favored customers, but Liana thought she detected a certain flirtatiousness in the young woman's smile. Which was understandable, Liana admitted to herself as they walked through the restaurant. Max was easily the best looking man in the place, and he was drawing admiring glances from a large portion of the female customers.

The "special" table turned out to be a richly uphol-stered booth, tucked in a quiet corner of the dining room. Fan-folded turquoise napkins accented the pale peach tablecloth, and the silver and crystal appeared to be top quality. The waiter presented them with leather-bound menus, then hurried off, promising to return promptly with their wine.

"I hope you don't mind," Max said, setting his menu aside. "I took the liberty of ordering champagne. The one they produce here is very good."

"Whatever you recommend," she replied, pretending an interest in the dinner selections printed on her menu. The ride to the restaurant had been fairly easy, because he'd begun talking about mundane things like the weather and agricultural development in the valley. But sitting across from Max in a romantically lit restaurant brought back his remark about "later."

After a long silence, his finger hooked over the edge of her menu, pulling it down until she had to meet his eyes. "Are you always this engrossed by food?"

Laughing nervously, she gave the list a last glance and set it aside. "I enjoy gourmet cooking. I've even experimented with it myself on occasion." She surveyed the room's elegant Southwestern decor. "John and I discussed opening a place like this at our winery, but after he died it just didn't happen."

"I've had the same thought about Valentin's," Max said. The waiter approached with their champagne and after he'd performed the little ceremony of opening and pouring, Max lifted his fluted glass and tilted it toward hers. "What shall we toast? The renewal of old friendships?"

Nodding, she touched her glass to his and took a sip. The champagne fizzed against her tongue like a Fourth-of-July sparkler, but its effect couldn't compare with what his next words did to her.

"And now," he said, raising his glass again, "let's drink to new beginnings." Something about his tone made her distinctly uneasy, but he anticipated her protest with, "That can mean mine, yours or your father's." After they'd sipped, he set the glass aside and faced her seriously. "How *is* your father, by the way?"

"Better than he was, but still a long way from complete recovery." She toyed with the slender stem of her wineglass. "The doctor said it was difficult to predict, given Dad's age and physical condition. He might be able to come home in a few weeks, if things go well."

"What will you do if he can't? Sybille said you didn't intend to stay here indefinitely."

"I didn't—don't. But at the moment I have my hands full with trying to get the place cleaned up and back on its feet financially. I haven't had time to make long-term plans."

Max gave her a worried frown. "But don't you think you should consider what will happen if you succeed? Your father's health wasn't the best before the accident, and his leg may take a long time to heal. Do you intend to stay until he's back on his feet?"

She pursed her mouth in annoyance. Why did everyone have to keep asking her that? She knew that saving the ranch wasn't the only problem she faced. But she wasn't going to admit—especially to Max—that the more she thought about it, the more hopeless it seemed. *Which is exactly what he wants me to think*, she realized with growing irritation. What a fool she'd been, letting him charm her into thinking that who they were didn't matter. The fact remained that their plans were in direct opposition. "Is that why you asked me to dinner? To remind me of all the problems I'm facing, in hopes that I'll give up and leave?"

He reached across the table to cover her hand with his own, making her realize she'd been drumming her fingers in agitation. "That's the last thing I want," he said fervently. "My plans for the land haven't changed, but my feelings for you have."

She closed her eyes, trying to ignore the tremor of warmth that ran through her. "This is wrong," she said, pulling her hand away. "I shouldn't even be here with you. It's like consorting with the enemy."

"That's crazy!" he protested. "I'm not your enemy. In fact, I've actually tried to be helpful. If you're honest with yourself, you can't deny that."

The problem was, he was right. Therein lay the most perplexing aspect of the situation—in addition to his talent for slipping right past her defenses. "I'm sorry, I didn't mean to sound ungrateful," she muttered.

"Then why don't we just forget our differences for a while and enjoy dinner?"

She looked into his eyes and read such sincerity there, she had to agree. The waiter arrived just then to take their orders, and when he left, Max quickly turned the conversation to wine making. Since it was a topic she knew well, Liana gradually began to relax.

They dined on Caesar salad and chicken Chardonnay—boneless chicken breast cooked in a delicately herbed white-wine sauce. For dessert there was white chocolate cheesecake. All of which, combined with the champagne, left Liana feeling deliciously sated and a bit drowsy. During the ride back to her father's house, she had to apologize twice for yawning.

"It isn't the company," she assured Max as he parked the truck under the oak trees.

"I'm glad to hear that." Smiling, he swiveled sideways to face her. His right arm rested on the back of the seat, and she thought she felt his fingers brush over the tightly confined hair at the back of her head. "Your hair is so beautiful. Why do you always wear it up?"

In the space of a moment, his tone had shifted from genial to sensual, and she felt an answering heat spring to life deep inside her. Distressed, she bent to retrieve her purse from the floor. "I don't wear it up all of the time. But usually it's easier to have it out of my way." She refrained from adding that she left it unbound when she went to bed.

"Do me a favor. Let it down."

Her heart started beating faster. "I—I don't think I should do that."

"Why not? I've seen it down before. Remember that first morning at the pond?"

Oh, yes, she remembered. Just as she recalled the look in his eyes when he'd seen her wet T-shirt. "I think I'd better go in now," she said, reaching for the door handle.

He caught her hand. "Wait. I'll get that for you." Without another word, he got out, opened the door on her side and walked her to the front porch.

Uncomfortable with the tension in the air, she avoided looking at him as she unlocked the door. But she had to face him to say good-night, and the barely restrained desire she saw in his eyes made her knees go weak.

"I want to kiss you again," he said, propping one hand on the doorjamb beside her head. In the porch light his features looked sharper than normal, giving him a lean, hungry look. "I want it so bad, I ache."

A frisson rippled down her spine as she remembered the sensation of his mouth against hers. In that moment she knew she wanted it, too. "You said it was my choice," she replied, stalling.

He leaned closer—so close she could have counted the dense black lashes that framed his eyes. "Then tell me not to do it."

She drew a breath, but the words wouldn't come. All she could do was stare, transfixed, as his eyelids began to droop sensually and his mouth moved nearer and nearer. At the last second, it was she who closed the millimeter of space remaining between them. The first touch of his lips brought pleasure so exquisite it bordered on pain. When he groaned and eased his arms around her, she melted against him. All restraint vanished as his mouth opened over hers hungrily. She felt the world begin to tilt and spin again, compelling her to wrap her arms around his waist.

After what seemed an eternity, he broke the contact just enough to whisper thickly, "Open your mouth for me, honey." When she complied, his tongue made a swift hot invasion, more erotic than anything she'd ever known, exploring with slow thrusts that caused a tightening deep in her belly. She moaned softly, and felt his hands begin to move urgently over her body, mold-ing her to him until she could feel the burning hardness of his erection, even through the layers of clothing that separated them. The reality of where they were headed suddenly intruded on the sensual fog she'd been floating in.

"Max, wait!" she gasped, when he paused. To her surprise, he loosened his embrace a little.

"Yeah, I know. Too much, too fast." He propped his chin on top of her head and swore softly. "Damn, lady. I've never known a woman who could do this to me. I promised myself I'd go slow for your sake, but you're really testing my self-control. Each taste of you makes me want more."

She moved her hands to his chest to put some space between them. "I'm not sure I'm ready for more."

He looked down at her, his eyes narrowing. "Your mind may not be, but your body sure is. Look at your breasts, Liana. Your nipples are so hard I can see them through your dress."

She didn't have to look down to know he was right. The sharp tingling she felt in her breasts told the whole story. Using her arms to cover herself, she tried to deny the obvious. "That doesn't necessarily mean I want to have sex."

"It isn't just sex," he retorted. He smoothed his hand down her back. "I want to make love with you. I want to give you so much pleasure, you'll forget all the bad things you learned about sex."

His words made her tremble. Apprehension wasn't the only emotion in play. Deep within her, she sensed a restlessness that felt almost like hunger. "Max, I'm not ready for this," she said in a shaky voice.

"I know." He cupped her chin with his hand, bringing their faces close once more. "Until next time, Liana," he murmured, just before his mouth pressed against hers in a brief, tender kiss. Then he released her, walked quickly to his truck, and drove off without looking back.

Dazed by the emotional turmoil she felt, Liana went inside and closed the door, then sagged back against it, unable to go farther. "Until next time," she whispered.

MAX STRODE BRISKLY through the moonlit vineyards, his destination the cool waters of the pond. *This could get to be a habit,* he thought wryly. At least until he found another way to ease his sexual frustration. Unfortunately, he wanted only one woman, and she wasn't ready for him yet.

He stopped to finger the tender young leaves on one vine. Funny, a short time ago he'd been so engrossed in his work he'd almost forgotten what it was like to burn with need for a woman. Liana had changed all that. He caught himself thinking about her almost constantly, his desire for her growing daily.

The bad news was, it was beginning to affect his efficiency, and he couldn't afford that. All around him the vines were sprouting; in a couple of months, clusters of tiny green grapes would appear. Before he knew it, harvest time would arrive, and he had a lot of work to do before then, including finding a way out of the hopeless situation between him and Frank Castillo.

And finding a way into his daughter's bed, he added to himself, continuing toward the pond. A shadow passed over him, and he glanced up to see the graceful flight of a barn owl. It swooped like some dark phantom in the direction of one of the nesting boxes that stood on tall poles around the perimeter of the vineyard. Max heard the keening cry of its young—undoubtedly waiting for their supper. *At least someone's hunger will be satisfied tonight,* he thought, sprinting the last distance to the water.

LIANA PAUSED IN THE doorway of her father's hospital room. "Hi, Dad. How's it going?"

His weathered face creased into a smile. "A lot better since they took my leg out of traction. The doc says I might be out of here in a few weeks."

She returned his smile and perched on the chair by the bed. "That's great news. You even *look* better today."

"Hospital food," he said with a chuckle. "Can't understand why people are always complaining about it. It tastes a load better than anything I could make. And my stomach trouble has all but cleared up." He squinted at her critically. "You, on the other hand, are looking a little peaked. Are you still wearing yourself out trying to clean up the ranch single-handed? I told you I didn't want you doing that."

"I'm okay," she assured him, wondering what his reaction would be if he knew her fatigue wasn't from work alone. There'd been too many nights lately when she'd tossed and turned in her bed, her sleep plagued with half-remembered dreams of a man with seductive blue eyes. After those kisses last night, she hadn't been able to sleep at all.

Her father didn't look convinced. "What have you been doing?"

"Oh, just a little sorting and reorganizing." As in the whole stable and several of the outbuildings, she added to herself. The man had acquired an incredible amount of junk over the years. "If you don't mind, I'd like to haul a few things away, as soon as J—" She bit the name off, remembering her father's dislike for the Mosers. "As soon as the truck's running again," she finished quickly.

"You're having it fixed? Who's doing the work?" He peered at her anxiously. "I don't like just anyone messing with it."

"Uh, he's supposed to be reliable. I checked at the garage where he used to work."

"What's his name? Maybe I know him."

Feeling trapped, Liana stammered, "Um—I—I don't remember." She'd never been able to lie to her father with any great success.

"You're hiding something. I can see it in your eyes. Come on, who is he?"

"Jeff Moser." She held up a hand as her father's expression began to harden. "Now, don't judge him by the name. He and Arlie were only cousins."

"Doesn't matter. Blood will tell. Those Mosers are bad news, all of them. And they've had it in for our family ever since the night Arlie and Rennie killed your sister."

Even though she didn't exactly harbor warm feelings for the family, his accusation seemed a bit extreme after twelve years. "Have they actually done anything since to make you feel that way?"

"They spread a lot of bad stories about you and Serena. And there were other incidents."

"Like what?"

He glanced away and began fiddling with the corner of the bedsheet. "I don't know... Just sneaky things that I couldn't prove. Most recently it was stuff like messing with my beehives and getting the bees all stirred up. Or teasing Sonny, until he was real upset. One time they spray-painted filthy words on my truck."

Liana began to get exasperated. This feud of his was beginning to sound more like a severe case of paranoia. "How can you be sure it was the Mosers? Did you catch them doing any of those things?"

"No, but it had to be them or Valentin, and he wasn't around when some of it happened."

"Dad, the things you're describing could have been high-school pranks. Lots of kids do things like that when they're bored and looking for mischief. Furthermore, Jeff has never been in any kind of trouble, from what I could determine. I even checked with the local sheriff's department before I hired him."

Her father's chin was set stubbornly. "I still don't like the idea of him being around."

Holding on to her growing impatience, she tried again to reason with him: "Look, he seems to be a nice guy who needs some work, and I need the help. You're the one who said I shouldn't be trying to run the place

myself. Jeff has offered to do some hauling for me, once
he's finished with the truck. Unless you can come up
with a better solution, I'm going to stay with mine."

He seemed to bridle at that, but then he let out a sigh
of defeat. "Okay, have it your way. But I still don't like
it. If I was on my feet, I wouldn't let a Moser within a
mile of my property, or my truck." He squinted at her
suspiciously. "Which reminds me of something else I've
been wondering about. How are you getting around?"

Groaning inwardly, she hedged, "I—uh, borrowed
a car."

"From who? Bartlett?"

Liana knew that George Bartlett owned the orange
groves to the east of her father's property, but she hadn't
met the man, so she didn't want to use him in a lie.
"Umm, no, not him."

"Who, then?"

Knowing he wouldn't give her any peace until she
told him, she sighed and said, "Oh, all right, it's Max's
car."

"Valentin!" her father exploded. "What in the world
are you doing with his car?"

"Using it to visit you, for one thing," she countered
irritably. "Please don't tell me again that he's the enemy."

"But he is, blast it. Loaning you a car is probably just
part of his plan to get his hands on my land. He probably figures he can sweet-talk you out of helping me."

His assumption deepened her irritation, even though
she'd assumed the same thing at one point. "That's ridiculous. Max offered me the use of his car with no

strings attached. If there had been, I wouldn't have accepted."

Her father shook his head, his expression mulish. "He's up to something, mark my words. Valentin is too ambitious to let that land go."

Without warning, she was reminded of Max's dream to expand Valentin Winery onto her father's property. What would he do if she succeeded, and her father bought out the lease? The possibility distressed her more than she would have believed. But at the same time, she felt a wave of guilt for the inherent disloyalty of her thoughts.

Unwilling to continue on that topic, Liana switched to another. "Speaking of your property, I can't approach the local banks about obtaining a loan until we decide what you intend to do with the place. I think your chances will be better if you tell them you're turning it into a boarding ranch." She didn't say how slim those chances were at the moment; he needed some encouraging news to keep him on the road to recovery.

She took her father's work-scarred hand and squeezed it gently. "Sonny just isn't bringing in any stud fees at the moment, and you can't afford to buy good brood mares for him. I know rebuilding Castillo's Arabians has been your dream, but sometimes dreams don't turn out the way we want."

Her father was regarding her with a soft gleam in his eyes. "You know, honey, when you were small you were such a timid little thing, you spooked if anyone looked at you. And here you are, reading me chapter and verse on how to pull myself out of the financial pit I've gotten myself into." He smiled slowly. "I guess all those years with Opal paid off."

Returning his smile, she agreed. "Your sister is a specialist when it comes to building backbone. I don't know what I would have done without her."

"You must be anxious to get back to Oregon to be with her and the others," he said, his smile fading.

Once again, his uncharacteristic vulnerability worried her. "You're my *father*," she reminded him. "I'll be happy to stay here as long as you need me." The assurance, impulsively spoken, brought a twinge of uncertainty. Could she live up to that promise?

"Would you, Liana?" He searched her expression urgently. "I know I don't have any right to ask, but—"

"You have every right. I . . ." A mist of tears blurred her vision. "I love you, Dad. You don't have to worry about me pining away for Oregon. Temecula was my first home, and in spite of the bad memories, it still feels like home." Again, she'd simply intended to reassure him, but in so doing she realized a startling truth: the place *was* beginning to feel like home, and even though she thought about Oregon from time to time, she didn't feel homesick.

Her father seemed to relax, although his voice was uneven when he said, "Thanks, honey. Your loyalty means a lot to me. Between us, we'll beat Valentin yet."

Valentin. Just the sound of his name made something inside her go soft and quivery. But at the same time, her conscience was pricked by a feeling of disloyalty. Her father would never understand if he learned of the effect Max had on her. She couldn't fully understand it herself. Fearing her reaction would show, she quickly changed the subject and steered clear of any mention of Max for the rest of her visit.

A THIN STRATUM OF clouds diffused the sun's heat as Liana exercised Sonny late that afternoon. Although he still acted skittish whenever she approached him, he'd allowed her to snap on a lunge line, and she'd talked him into cantering around the paddock. She kept her attention sharply focused on the temperamental beast, but when Max's truck started up the drive, she recognized it instantly. By the time he came to a stop outside the paddock, she'd slowed Sonny to a cool-down walk.

Max parked the truck and came to lean on the gate, his smile admiring. "So, you've got him under your spell now, too."

"Not really," she said, turning her gaze back to Sonny. Looking at Max was far too stimulating. "I think he was just so bored he would have let anyone exercise him."

"You underestimate yourself, my dear."

That queer shaky feeling sprang to life again in the pit of her stomach. "What he really needs is to be ridden hard," she replied, sidestepping his comment. "It might take a little of the pepper out of him. But I don't have a strong enough death wish to attempt it."

"Let me try. He didn't seem to mind when I groomed him."

"Absolutely not. My father's the only one who's been able to ride him. If you got thrown, I'd never forgive myself."

"You hear that, Sonny? She cares." Max opened the gate and approached the stallion, who came to meet him as docilely as a pet lamb. He grasped the horse's halter and led him over to Liana. "Tell you what, I'll try saddling him. If that doesn't upset him, we'll proceed from there."

"Max, I really don't think you should," she protested, but he'd already begun guiding Sonny toward the stable, and she had no choice but to follow. Inside, Max saddled the horse with a confidence that allayed some of her fears. Sonny barely noticed when Max swung up into the saddle, he did it with such natural grace. When Max urged him into a walk, the stallion pranced a little, but seemed to accept the mastery of his rider. They seemed to move as one—the powerful, spirited stallion and the man who commanded him. Liana caught herself staring openmouthed at the beautiful picture they made.

After a few circuits of the paddock, Max reined in and said, "Why don't we saddle one of the horses you board here and go for a ride?"

"You did that so easily," she commented. "You must've had some riding experience since we were kids."

He grinned and shrugged. "A little. I'll tell you about it if you'll come riding with me."

She hadn't had time for any riding since she'd been back, and the idea appealed to her so much, she agreed.

They set out over the gentle hills bordering her father's property, slowly at first, then picking up speed. The air was full of the fresh scent of spring, and the wind tugged playfully at their hair, tousling Max's dark waves and loosening Liana's neat bun. Sonny and the bay gelding Liana had chosen, cantered along companionably for a while, then slowed to a walk again, giving their riders a chance to talk.

"Okay, tell me how you came to be such an expert horseman," Liana demanded.

Max laughed. "I'm not, really. I had a little experience in France, because my uncle had horses, but most of what I know, I learned from watching your father years ago. He was such a great rider. I hope his injury doesn't end his riding days for good."

A little pall of worry fell over her. "The doctor just said we'd have to wait and see."

Max leaned over to take her hand and squeeze it. "Frank's a tough old guy. I think he'll be all right." He tapped her nose teasingly. "I brought you out here to get away from your worries, and now look what I've done. Tell you what, let's have a race. Say, from here to the back fence of the paddock. That should give you something else to think about."

She laughed in spite of her concern for her father. "Some race that would be. Sonny could beat this guy by a mile." She gave the bay's withers an apologetic pat. "No offense, pal."

"I'll give you a head start. How about from that tree down the road? That should even things out." He teased her with a grin. "Unless you're chicken."

She glared at him and reached to resecure the pins holding her hair. "All right, you're on. What does the winner get?"

"If you win, there's a case of Valentin wine in my truck that's yours. If I win . . ." A wicked gleam lit his eyes. "Well, I'll think of something."

"Don't think too hard," she told him, starting her horse down the dirt road with a little kick. "If your wine is the prize, I'll win if I have to carry the horse."

Adrenaline began to surge through her veins as she reached the tree Max had indicated. Immediately she urged her mount to a gallop, deliberately not checking to see if Max was ready to begin. With the element of a surprise start, she might be able to beat him. A wild exhilaration swept over her as she and the bay thundered down the road. She'd forgotten the sheer joy of racing with a powerful beast beneath her.

The wind tore at her hair, loosening more pins. Her long tresses began to whip free, but she ignored them. She hadn't ridden this fast in ages, and just staying in the saddle required her full attention. They were within sight of the stable when she heard the pounding of Sonny's hooves behind her. She tried urging her mount to speed up, but Sonny and his grinning rider pulled abreast of her, then plunged ahead just as they reached the back fence of the paddock.

Giddy and slightly breathless, she tightened the reins, slowing her horse to a walk. Max pulled the stallion in, too, and circled around until he was beside her again. Looking exultant, Max exclaimed, "That was great, wasn't it? Really makes you feel alive."

She nodded, but couldn't resist teasing him. "Even though I was horribly outclassed."

He sent her a smoldering look. "Sweetheart, no one could outclass you. Do you have any idea how beautiful you look with your hair down?"

Sensual heat bloomed within her. She quickly looked away and made herself flippantly reply, "You're just saying that to make me feel better about losing a case of wine."

"I might give it to you anyway," he said as they reached the yard in front of the stable and dismounted.

"That offer sounds as if it comes with conditions." Conditions she didn't dare think about. She tied her horse and began unsaddling it.

Following her example, Max unhitched Sonny's girth and said, "The only condition is that you don't renege on my reward for winning."

"You haven't told me what that is, yet." Not anxious to hear his reply, she pulled the saddle off the horse's back and headed for the stable with it. To her chagrin, Max followed right behind her with Sonny's saddle. But he didn't speak until the gear had been stowed in the tack room.

As she turned to leave, he caught her shoulder, bringing her around to face him in the dim, cool interior of the stable. "This is what I want," he murmured, sliding his fingers through her hair and pulling her closer. His warm mouth closed over hers with stunning urgency. An answering need flared inside her before she had time to think.

His hands tangled in her hair, drawing her head back to give him better access to her mouth. He kissed her until she was gasping and trembling, then his hands moved again, riding down the curve of her back and hips. He pressed himself against her body, letting her feel the effect she had on him, gently grinding his arousal into the softness of her belly.

She moaned in protest when he backed away. For the first time she found herself wanting more—needing more. Max responded by cupping her breasts with his hands, massaging slowly. Mere need exploded into something much more powerful. His hands moved down to the hem of her T-shirt. "Max," she gasped, as his fingers slid up under the fabric to caress her naked skin.

"What?" he replied huskily, kissing her again, then using his warm moist mouth to trace the curve of her throat. Distracted, she barely noticed as he fumbled briefly with the front catch of her bra. But when the confining cups fell away and his hands captured her naked flesh, the sweet shock of it made her cry out. He went still, holding her gently. "Am I frightening you, Liana?" he asked hoarsely.

She knew that if she said yes, he'd stop, but that was the last thing she wanted. "No, that's not it," she admitted, her voice trembling. "I . . . I just didn't expect it to feel so . . ." Words failed her in the heady swirl of sensation.

A soft growl of satisfaction rumbled in his throat. "It's going to feel better than this," he promised. She gasped as his fingertips lightly traced over her nipples, making them contract until they almost hurt.

"Max, please . . ."

"What would you like, honey? Do you want to feel my mouth there? Because I'm dying to taste your lovely breasts." When she nodded, he eased away from her a bit, and she felt cool air touch her feverish skin as he slid her shirt off. Then he bent his head, and she cried out again as his hot mouth imprisoned the aching tip of her breast.

Her knees buckled, and she would have collapsed to the floor if his strong arm hadn't caught her securely around the waist. Mindlessly she burrowed her fingers into his dark hair and arched her back, as he pleasured her to a point where she didn't think she could bear it. And yet, she craved more. Tightening her grip on his hair, she tugged his head up and tried to voice her need, but she couldn't find the words.

"I know, honey," he said, breathing raggedly. "It's not enough, is it?" He shifted his stance, bringing her upright as he backed toward the support beam of one of the empty stalls. Bracing against it, he drew her toward him. "Come here, love, and I'll show you how good passion can be."

She let him pull her close until her naked breasts were crushed deliciously against his chest, and her lower body rode the muscular hardness of his thigh. When he grasped her hips, rocking her against him, her insides went wild, quivering and jumping in waves of liquid heat. With a little sob, she collapsed into his arms, clinging helplessly as the small storm raged within her.

When it was over, he held her for long moments, whispering softly into her ear, telling her how beautiful and sexy she was. But as the sensual fog enshrouding her began to clear, a distressing thought pierced her consciousness. She'd been completely vulnerable to him during that passionate little interval, and that sense of losing control stirred old fears to life. She couldn't afford to let any man have that much power over her.

She pushed away from him, disentangling their legs and covering her breasts with her arms.

"Liana, what—?" Max looked dumbfounded.

Painfully aware of her nakedness, she turned her back on him and began searching for her shirt. When his hands wrapped around her upper arms, she tensed. "Don't touch me."

"Why not? Just when I think we're making some progress you shove me away. I want to know what happened."

She wrenched away from him and continued looking for her shirt. "I came to my senses." She spied the missing garment and snatched it up. As she pulled it on, she heard Max swear softly. When she turned to face him, frustration had darkened his expression.

"I think you're running away because you're scared by what just happened to you," he charged quietly.

She lifted her chin. "I'm not afraid of you."

"No. You're afraid of yourself—and what you feel when I touch you."

She forced out a laugh. "You overestimate yourself."

He took a step toward her. "Really? Let me kiss you again and let's see what happens."

She backed away so fast, she nearly tripped over her own feet. "Don't you dare."

He grimaced wryly. "You see? I was right about your being afraid." He spread his arms placatingly. "But there's nothing to fear. You seemed to enjoy yourself a few minutes ago." His eyes smoldered with promise. "I have a feeling it'll be even better when we make love." The thought of actually making love with him sent a tremor through her. Instinctively, she knew it would go far beyond the passionate abandon she'd just experienced. Yet, even as she acknowledged that daunting prospect, a perverse flicker of curiosity teased her. "We aren't going to make love," she declared, as much to herself as to him.

He raised an eyebrow in challenge. "Maybe not today, but it's going to happen eventually. You just need a little more time to get used to the idea." He turned abruptly and stepped into the tack room, reappearing a moment later with the grooming implements.

Nonplussed by his sudden departure, she demanded, "Where do you think you're going with those?"

"To groom the horses," he said, heading past her to the door. "It's the best cure I know for frustration—other than that ice-cold pond of yours. And right now my frustration level is at an all-time high."

"It's going to stay that way," she warned, following him outside.

He turned to give her a piercing look. "Want to bet on that?"

"I don't gamble, even if it's a sure thing." Casting him a disparaging look, she continued on toward the house. But she couldn't escape a feeling that the odds were heavily stacked in his favor.

7

DAYLIGHT HAD JUST BEGUN to outline the eastern horizon when the telephone's shrill ringing yanked Liana out of a troubled dream. Groaning softly, she rolled out of bed and staggered to the extension in the upstairs hallway. After a stifled yawn, she muttered, "Hello." But her senses snapped to attention when Max's deep voice came over the line.

"I woke you, didn't I? I'm sorry, honey. But I wanted to talk to you before I left."

He was leaving? She tried to ignore the sinking feeling in her stomach as she made herself inquire coolly, "Where are you going?"

"To a wine competition in Napa. I'll be gone a week. I intended to tell you yesterday, but as you'll recall, you went into the house and wouldn't speak to me after our little—uh—encounter in the stable." He hesitated and then added, "Did you find the wine?"

He'd left the case on the back porch, after grooming both horses and turning them loose in separate paddocks. "Yes, but you shouldn't have. I didn't win the race."

His voice lowered sexily. "Yeah. But the reward you gave me was a real stunner."

Embarrassment flooded through her, making her feel as if she were blushing all over. "That was a mistake," she said shakily. "One I don't intend to repeat."

"Wrong. It was perfect and right. And I loved every minute of it." He chuckled softly. "Even if I did need a cold shower afterward."

"Max, I'm serious!" she insisted.

"So am I. The next time we're together, I'm going to show you just how serious I am. Grooming horses and cold showers are only temporary cures. I still want you so bad, I can taste it."

Once more, the sensual power of his words engulfed her, and she had to close her eyes and lean back against the wall. Dimly she heard him say, "Goodbye, Liana. I'll call you from Napa." Uttering a soft exasperated sound, she hung up the phone and went to get dressed.

She was just pouring her second cup of coffee when a knock sounded on the kitchen door. When she opened it, Jeff stood there looking uneasy.

"I hope I'm not disturbing you too early," he began, fiddling with the baseball cap he held. "But I went by the garage on the way over, and I'm afraid I've got bad news on the truck."

Repressing an urge to groan aloud, she said, "You're not disturbing me. Would you like to come in for a cup of coffee?"

He flushed and shook his head. "Thanks, but I can't stay. I just wanted to tell you that the parts I needed for your dad's truck are on back order, and they don't know how long it'll take to get them in. In the meantime, I've got some other jobs I can take on, unless you have something for me to do here."

Liana sighed. She'd been counting on having the truck to start hauling away some of her father's accumulated junk before she approached the banks. There was a good chance that they would want to look at the property before they made a decision on a loan. Swallowing her disappointment, she said, "I'm sorry, I don't have anything else for you at the moment. But I'd appreciate it if you'd let me know as soon as those parts come in."

He nodded apologetically. "Sure thing. And . . . I'm sorry about the delay."

"Don't be." She reassured him with a smile. "It isn't your fault."

But that didn't change the fact that her plans had developed another snag, she thought, as Jeff retreated from the door. She drank her coffee and brooded at the kitchen table for a few minutes, then sat up with new determination. The cleanup side of this project might be delayed, but she could still work on the financial part. Settling at her father's desk, she began assembling a business proposal to take around to the local banks. By dinnertime, she'd come up with an inventive, if highly optimistic, plan to bring Castillo's Arabians back into the black. The trick would be convincing a loan officer that her plan had a prayer of succeeding, she decided. Rubbing her tired eyes, she headed for the kitchen to fix something for lunch.

Max's call caught her in the midst of putting together pasta primavera. "I wish I were there with you," he said as soon as she picked up the receiver.

Her pulse jumped into double time. "Hello, Max."

He moaned. "Do you have any idea how sexy it sounds when you say my name with that breathless little catch in your voice?" He sighed in frustration. "If there'd been any way to get out of this trip, I would have."

She sat down at the kitchen table and tried to collect herself. "You've got to stop talking to me like that," she said, attempting a firm tone.

"Why?"

"Because..." She floundered, unable to think clearly amid the riot of emotions he'd stirred up.

"Because it reminds you of how it felt when I kissed you?" he suggested.

Pressing a hand to her forehead, she tried to block the images he'd called forth. "I don't want to hear this."

"Fine. What would you like to talk about?"

His sudden acquiescence caught her off guard. "I...I don't know."

"Did you try any of the wine I gave you?"

"Not yet," she admitted. She was having a hard enough time not thinking about him. The seductive taste of his wine would be sure to keep the memories alive.

"Then have some tonight. Think of me as you drink it," he urged quietly. "Good night, Liana. I'll call you tomorrow." With that, he hung up.

He called the next night, and the next, his voice reaching out to touch her almost as tangibly as his hands and mouth had. And even though she knew she shouldn't listen, she couldn't bring herself to hang up on him. When he didn't call the fourth night, the hours dragged by as if on leaden feet.

DARK THUNDERCLOUDS CREPT across the sky as Liana urged her mount, a roan gelding, into a trot. Since her ride with Max a week before, she'd started taking out the horses boarded at the ranch, a practice her father backed wholeheartedly. "They could use some riding during the week, especially since their owners only show up on the weekends," he told her.

What she didn't tell him was the real reason she needed these rides. Ever since Max had left, she'd been filled with a nervous energy that never let up, no matter how hard she worked. His phone calls had made it even worse. Horseback riding was the only thing she'd found that brought some relief from her restlessness. Which was why she'd ventured out on the roan, even though a storm had been predicted.

Thunder rumbled in the distance and the wind picked up, whipping loose strands of her hair. She was at the northwest corner of her father's property, where he kept his beehives in a stand of oak trees. Just a little to the west were Max's vineyards, and although she knew he wasn't due back from Napa until the following day, her attention kept straying to the fence that separated the properties.

Lightning flashed nearby, and the roan snorted and danced sideways. "You're right, fella," she said, patting his neck reassuringly. "It's time to head for home." She urged him into a canter, following the dirt track that ran along the property line. By the time she'd neared the pond, the storm had arrived in full force, bringing a torrent of rain.

A bright flash just ahead of her signaled another lightning strike dangerously close, and the resulting sharp crack and boom caused the roan to rear in fright. Grabbing the saddle horn, she barely managed to maintain her seat. When he landed on all four feet again, she had to pull on the reins hard to keep him from bolting. Because she had to keep wiping the rain out of her eyes, she couldn't see well enough to risk a fast trip back to the stable. For that same reason, she nearly rode straight into the power pole that lay propped across her path, its wires tangled with a smaller pole that had fallen beside it.

Thankful that she'd seen it in time, she started to guide her horse around the mess, but then stopped when a fluttering movement caught her eye. An owl's nesting box lay in the mud and next to it were two tiny owlets, their downy white feathers drenched. One was deathly still, but the other seemed to be struggling valiantly for its life.

With a soft cry, Liana dismounted and tied the roan to the fence. Then she carefully approached the small bird. When it saw her it hissed so loudly, she could hear the sound over the racket of the storm. "Hey, little one, I'm not going to hurt you," she said in a soothing monotone. The owlet raised its stubby wings and hissed again, its huge dark eyes glowing fiercely in its circular face.

"Is that any way to talk to the lady who's trying to save you?" she queried gently, easing nearer. After briefly sizing up the situation, she decided the only solution would be to scoop the feisty creature into the nesting box and carry it back to the house that way. Grateful she'd worn riding gloves, she moved in cautiously and picked up the box. The owlet tried to flounder away from her, but the mud impeded its progress. She succeeded in capturing it on the third try, and once she'd placed it inside the deep box, it couldn't escape.

"All right, my ferocious feathered friend," she muttered, awkwardly balancing the box as she climbed back into the saddle. "Let's get out of here." The ride back to the stable seemed to take an eternity, and she was soaked to the skin by the time she led the roan inside. But she didn't give a thought to her own comfort until the horse had been unsaddled and rubbed down— a feat she had to accomplish by the light of a propane lantern, since the power had been knocked out. Apparently the fallen electricity pole had supplied the ranch. Also, her attempts to start the generator had proved futile. Like so many things on the ranch, it appeared to have fallen into disrepair.

At last, clutching the nesting box, she made a dash through the pouring rain for the darkened house. Once inside, her first priority was getting a fire started in the living-room hearth. There was an old gas furnace, but

it seemed wasteful to turn it on for just one person.
"And one owlet," she added, setting the box down on
the rug in front of the fireplace.

The fire caught quickly, sending a warm welcoming
glow into the room. Liana sat back on her heels before
the flickering flames and smiled. Her enjoyment was
interrupted by a strange sound coming from the box,
not unlike that of someone aggressively slurping soup.
She peered in at her tiny ward who was craning his
short neck around frantically. "I guess that means
you're hungry. But I'm a little low on rodents at the
moment."

She was considering alternate menu options when
someone knocked hard on the back door. Peering out
the kitchen window, she saw a hulking figure wearing
a dripping-wet black poncho. The hood was pulled
forward, obscuring the wearer's face, and in the gray
half-light the effect was vaguely sinister.

"Who is it?" she queried as forcefully as she could
manage.

The figure turned, pushing back the hood, and Max's
stunning face came into view. "It's me, honey. I came
to see if you were all right."

"Max!" Relief washed over her as she flung open the
door. "I'm sorry. For a moment there, I didn't know it
was you. You weren't supposed to be back until tomorrow."

His wonderful smile appeared, lighting his face and
kindling a glow of happiness in her heart. "I know. I left
early. The judging was over, and I had urgent business
waiting for me back here."

She paused uncertainly in the act of waving him inside. "Oh. Does that mean you don't have time to come in and tell me about the competition?" A sharp pang of disappointment pierced her elation, making her realize just how much she wanted him to stay.

"I have all the time in the world." He sobered and gazed at her intently. "You're the reason I came back early."

Liana felt as if she'd been zapped by the downed power line. Sensual energy surged through her, overriding reasonable thought processes, leaving her unable to respond.

He stared at her for a moment longer, then checked himself. "But before we go into that—" he nodded toward the gloomy interior of the house "—my power's out and it looks as if yours is, too. Would you like me to see if I can get your generator running? The storm probably knocked down some wires and it could be some time before anyone gets out to fix them."

She nodded, marshaling her swirling senses to formulate an answer. "Lightning hit one of the poles between our properties. I was out riding and nearly ran into it. One of your nesting boxes was knocked down, too."

He winced. "So that's why you're all wet. I hope there weren't any owls in it."

"Unfortunately, there were. Two nestlings. One was dead, but I brought the other home with me. He seems to be a fighter, so he might make it."

"Good. We'll take care of him as soon as I get you some electricity. Is the generator still at the back of the stable?"

"Yes. But you'll probably be wasting your time. I couldn't get it started."

He scowled in mock reproof. "Have a little faith in me. I've been known to have a magic touch when it comes to machinery."

And everything else, she thought.

He eyed her critically, then added, "In the meantime, I think you'd better get into some dry clothes. As much as I love the wet-T-shirt-look on you, it could be detrimental to your health."

She looked down at herself and groaned. Even though she was wearing a bra this time, her damp shirt clung closely to her curves. When she lifted her gaze again, however, Max was already dashing back to his truck through the heavy rain. She heard him drive off toward the stable as she closed the door and hurried upstairs to change.

The soft pink sweat suit she hastily pulled on offered more in the line of comfort and warmth than feminine allure, even if it did have a wide neckline that tended to slip off the shoulder. She was in the process of hitching it up when she caught sight of herself in the bathroom mirror. Even in the dim light available, she could see her sodden hair had drooped out of its normal tidy knot, giving her a wild, unkempt look. Distressed that Max had seen her like that, she yanked the pins out and grabbed a comb and brush before going back downstairs.

The flames crackled and popped in the living-room fireplace as she sat before it on an old wedding-ring quilt. She'd towel-dried her long hair and now was endeavoring to comb the tangles out of it. The nesting box stood to one side of the hearth, and her small visitor was making a tremendous racket with his odd slurping sounds. The only time he ceased was when she came within sight, and then it was only to hiss at her.

She'd nearly finished untangling her hair when Max knocked on the kitchen door again. Reluctant to leave the warmth of the fire, she called for him to come in. She heard him moving around in the kitchen, ridding himself of his poncho and shoes. Then he appeared in the doorway, wearing dark slacks and a blue V-neck sweater that was the exact shade of his eyes. He looked thoroughly disgusted with himself.

"I hope you're into candlelight." He crossed the room and sat down next to her on the soft quilt. "Because even I couldn't fix that generator. It must have rusted solid, years ago."

Who needed electricity, Liana wondered, when he could illuminate a room just by walking into it? Impulsively, she reached out to touch his arm and felt the hard warmth of muscle under the soft fabric. "You tried, and I appreciate that."

He looked down at her hand, then covered it with his own. "Enough to let me stay for a while? I don't want to risk driving home while it's raining so hard."

She drew a quick breath. Ostensibly he was asking for shelter from the storm, but she knew that by allowing him to stay, she would be opening the door to much more. The decision didn't take more than a moment. "You're welcome to stay," she said gently.

His hand tightened over hers and he let out a slow breath. "I was hoping you'd say that." He started to lean toward her, a slightly dreamy look softening his eyes. Her pulse leaped into a wild dance in anticipation of his kiss, but the owlet chose that moment to increase the volume of his noisemaking.

A last vestige of uncertainty made her seize the excuse to back away. "I think he's hungry." She gently withdrew her hand and nodded in the direction of the nesting box.

Max sighed and moved over to peer inside. "Poor little thing," he murmured. Amazingly, the creature didn't hiss. "I hope his parents are sheltered in a tree somewhere. I'll put the box back up after the storm. If they're still around, they'll return to him. For now, we'll have to improvise on feeding him." He sent her a teasing grin. "I don't suppose you have any dead rats or mice lying around?"

She wrinkled her nose in distaste. "No. And I'm fresh out of owl chow too."

"How about some raw chicken breast, then?"

"You're in luck. That happens to be part of my diet."

He followed her into the kitchen, and took over the job of boning and slicing the meat. Then he took it back into the living room and patiently fed small pieces, one at a time, to the baby owl. All the while, he spoke in a low-pitched litany that seemed to calm it.

Fascinated, Liana sat a short distance away to observe. As she watched Max's gentle interaction with the small bird, a piercing tenderness assailed her, adding yet another aspect to the whirl of emotions he stirred in her.

When he turned unexpectedly and looked at her, she felt as if she were drowning in the deep azure of his eyes. "I think your little friend will go to sleep if we cover the box," he said quietly. Wordlessly she handed him the towel she'd brought down earlier to dry her hair. After he'd covered the box, he eased over until he was next to her again. "Now, how about a little sustenance for us?"

Another rush of excitement jolted her. Did he mean . . . ? "Like what?" she asked breathlessly.

He smiled and reached to trace the curve of her cheek with a fingertip. "Why don't we start with a glass of my wine?" One eyebrow rose in playful inquiry. "Unless, of course, you drank it all."

"No. There's a bottle in the refrigerator." When she rose to get it, he followed her once again. The storm had blocked out the last faint light of day, and they had to use a flashlight to find their way around the kitchen. As he opened the wine, and she collected glasses and some candles, the dim lighting magnified her awareness of his dynamic presence.

Back in the living room, they lit a few candles and settled in front of the fireplace, sitting face-to-face, Indian-style. Max poured the wine, then proposed a toast. "To rainstorms." He clinked his goblet against hers and took a drink.

She stared at him, bemused. "Rainstorms?"

He smiled lazily. "Yeah. If it weren't for this one, I probably wouldn't be sitting here drinking wine with the most beautiful woman in the world."

She blushed and took a sip of the wine to cover her discomposure. It was her favorite, the sauvignon blanc, and the flavor shimmered on her taste buds. Closing her eyes to prolong the sensation, she waited a moment, then swallowed.

Her eyes popped open again when Max uttered a low growl. He was watching her closely. "If you're trying to seduce me, sweetheart, you're headed in the right direction."

"I wasn't—"

He belayed her protest with an upraised hand. "I know you weren't. You're just naturally sensual."

Panic made her fingers tighten on the goblet's stem. "No, I'm not," she replied unsteadily. "That's the problem."

He gently loosened her death grip on the glass. "Easy, love. We're not going to rush into anything." He picked up the hairbrush she'd left lying on the rug. "Why don't you just relax and let me brush your hair?"

Self-consciously, she touched a long dark strand that had slipped over her shoulder. It was nearly dry, from the heat of the fire. "You don't have to. I've already combed most of the tangles out."

"I wasn't worrying about tangles." He placed his hands on her shoulders and lightly twisted her around until her back was to him. She felt his fingers thread through to her scalp and comb downward. "Your hair is like the finest black silk. I'd like to spend the rest of my life just running my fingers through it." He eased her backward until she was nestled between his hard thighs. His fingertips massaged her head, and slid down again. "Or feeling it brush over my skin."

The erotic images *that* called forth made her shiver. She felt the brush's bristles sink into her heavy tresses and stroke to the ends again…and again…and again, until she was awash in pleasure. Only then did he lay the brush aside and pull her close to lie in the crook of his arm.

"You're purring, love," he said, his voice rich with masculine satisfaction. He plucked the wineglass from her hand and set it on a nearby table. "I think it's time for phase two."

8

"PHASE TWO?" As she lay cradled in Max's arm, Liana gazed up at him through a pleasant fog of contentment. Her sweatshirt had slipped completely off one shoulder, and she absently tried to shove it up.

"Mmm-hmm." He reached over and deliberately pushed the neckline of the sweatshirt back down, then bent to place his warm mouth on her bare skin. Pleasure flowed over her in waves. When she moaned and twisted around to give him better access, his hand closed over her breast, massaging gently, and the feeling intensified.

Threading her fingers through his coal-dark hair, she tugged his head up until she could gaze into his eyes. They had a dreamy sensuality that made her pulse quicken. "Max," she breathed. "Please kiss me."

His mouth brushed over hers with the tantalizing beauty of a glissando. "I have a better idea. Why don't *you* kiss *me*?"

She hesitated a moment, then raised her head to press her parted lips against his. He didn't help her, although his mouth molded and clung to hers as she angled this way and that with nibbling little kisses. But when she stroked the seam of his mouth with the tip of her tongue, he groaned and became more aggressive.

Gently imprisoning her tongue, he coaxed her to taste the slick warmth inside his mouth. His tongue felt like velvet as he guided her into a kind of love play she'd never imagined. When he reversed the game and invaded her mouth with deep hunger, a wild yearning for more and more swept through her.

She wrapped her arms around him, straining closer, but he tore his mouth away and buried his face against her neck, his breath blasting hot on her skin. "I can't believe what you do to me with a kiss. We've just started, and I'm ready for phase four already."

"Phase four?" she asked breathlessly.

He raised his head to look at her, his eyes slightly glazed. "You'll find out when we get there."

His hand slid up inside the front of her shirt and she gasped as he found the sensitive curve of her breast.

"You're so soft, so lovely," he murmured. "I want to see you, to touch all of you." He eased her to a sitting position. "Sweetheart, will you take your top off for me?"

She felt a pinprick of uncertainty, but the smoldering need she saw in his eyes compelled her to grasp the hem of the shirt and pull it over her head. The warmth from the fireplace was no match for the blazing heat she felt as Max's gaze roved over her naked breasts.

He didn't give her time to feel self-conscious. Cupping her shoulders with his hands, he eased her back on the puffy softness of the quilt, then yanked off his sweater and stretched out beside her.

Her own nakedness temporarily forgotten, she stared in fascination at the muscular perfection of his chest.

A light mat of black hair swirled over his smooth skin in precise patterns, converging to a narrow strip that bisected his flat abdomen and disappeared under the waistband of his slacks.

"Is this phase three?" she asked, then inhaled sharply as he bent to taste the rosy tips of her breasts.

"Mmm, not quite," he mumbled against her skin. Her nipples felt tingly and hot, and when he drew one deep into his mouth she experienced an exquisite contraction low in her body. As he gently sucked, she felt as if she were being drawn tighter and tighter, until she feared she might snap.

"Max, please. I need . . ."

He lifted his head to look into her eyes. His hand moved down to the ache between her thighs. "Does this help, love?" He began to rub in slow circles, and she let out a soft guttural sound at the voluptuous pleasure that coursed through her, bringing with it an insatiable desire for more.

"It helps and makes things worse at the same time." It also made her feel as if she were losing all control of herself. But somehow she didn't care.

He smiled with poignant empathy. "I know. That's what happens to me every time I kiss you or touch you." He stroked harder and a shiver ran through her. When she cried out his name again, he knelt beside her and slid off her pink sweatpants and cotton briefs with one smooth motion.

"Phase three?" she asked shakily.

His laugh held a deep sexy note as he lay back down, pulling her on top of him. "I didn't intend to make this sound like a scientific process. I've never felt less scientific in my life." He hugged her close, rubbing the silky mat of his chest hair against her breasts, and she couldn't remember anything ever feeling quite so wonderful. He clasped the backs of her knees, guiding them apart until she was straddling him and intimately pressed against his hard flat stomach. Each time he took a breath, his warm smooth skin connected with her in a shockingly sensual caress.

Bracing her hands on his shoulders, she pushed up to a sitting position, which only served to increase the tantalizing contact of their lower bodies. She hadn't felt so open and vulnerable in a long time—maybe never. Because what she felt went far beyond mere physical sensation.

"It's your turn now," he said. He took her hands and placed them on his chest. "Touch me, Liana, like I touched you."

She complied, shyly at first, then with more abandon as she discovered the wonderful combination of hard bone and vibrant muscle that made him male. Two silky locks of her hair slithered forward to frame her face and he reached to stroke them against her breasts. "You're so beautiful," he said with quiet intensity, then moaned when her fingers brushed over one of his nipples.

"So are you." On sheer instinct, she bent and tasted the small brown disk. He groaned aloud and ran his hands up her thighs to grip her bottom. Then he gently shoved her back until she was positioned right over the fly of his slacks. The layers of fabric did nothing to neutralize the heat and hardness of his erection, and when he tightened his hold on her and ground into her softness, the glorious friction kindled a flame in her that grew hotter every second. Everything else began to fade into insignificance as her whole being focused on that insatiable, burning need.

When he stopped moving and pulled her to his chest into a brief embrace, she uttered a sharp protest. He spoke with difficulty. "Hang on, sweetheart. I've got a couple of things to take care of before this goes any further." He carefully rolled her to the floor, and she watched, transfixed, as he quickly rid himself of his slacks and pulled a wallet out of the back pocket. Even though she'd occasionally glimpsed her late husband's unclothed body, he'd never been blatant about exposing her to his nakedness—not like this. Nor had he been quite so . . . substantial.

Max was dauntingly aroused and he made no effort to hide it as he took a small packet from his wallet. A part of her wanted to look away, but a stronger, more elemental urge kept her gaze fixed on him as he efficiently donned the filmy sheath.

Apparently her expression revealed some of her misgivings, because he smiled reassuringly as he returned and took her into his arms. "Your eyes are as big as saucers. Are you afraid I'll hurt you?" He tilted her face up for a lingering kiss. "Because I won't. We'll take things as slow as you need." He laughed ruefully. "I just hope I don't die in the process, because I can't remember ever being this hard." He smoothed one hand down her side. "I want to be inside you so much, I hurt."

She tensed as his fingers probed between her thighs, finding the ache that still throbbed there, bringing her back to smoldering need almost instantly. When she whimpered his name, he pulled her astride him again and clasped her hips. "Take me inside you, love. Before I expire." With a naturalness that sent her senses reeling, his body merged with hers.

Her breath caught, and she shuddered at the totality of his invasion. She felt as if he'd taken possession of her, body and soul, and she shuddered again as he moved beneath her, his hands guiding her in an irresistible dance that brought the fire within her to white-hot. Slowly at first, then faster and faster, they moved together until she didn't think she could bear another second of the intense pleasure without flying apart.

Then she heard his voice, raspy with desire. "Don't fight it love, let go. Let it happen." He touched her where the fire seemed to be centered, and her world burst into a million shimmering fragments. In the midst of her ecstasy, she felt Max arch up into her one last time with a shout of release.

Contentment washed over Max as he lay recovering in the glow of the flickering firelight. He felt utterly drained, yet complete. Liana's limp form was sprawled gracefully atop him, and he stroked her with tenderness, enjoying the satin-smooth texture of her back and sweetly rounded hips. He could still see how beautiful she'd looked at the zenith of her climax, her head thrown back, her hair cascading over her shoulders. That choked little scream she'd uttered was the sexiest sound he'd ever heard. It made him want to bring her to that point of abandon again and again.

Her hair lay over his chest in a silken black tangle, and when he combed his fingers through it, she moaned. "Am I still alive?"

He chuckled softly, his heart swelling with affection. "Yes. From what I've heard, very few people expire from *la petite mort*."

She raised her head and studied him with dazed eyes. "What?"

"That's what the French call it—'the little death.'" He lifted a lock of her hair and draped it over her shoulder. "Until now, I thought they were exaggerating."

Her brow knit in puzzlement. "Oh, come on. You don't expect me to believe you've never . . . Well . . . you know . . . before."

He smiled at her lingering reserve. "Not like this. Climaxes vary in degree for men, just as they do for women. What we just shared was the best."

A little grin tugged at her mouth as she laid her head back on his chest. "Okay, you've proved to me that I can be a wanton woman. What's phase five? A memorial service?"

"No. Next you decide whether you want to move to a bed, or stay here all night."

Her head popped up again, and she shoved her hair out of her eyes. "Does that mean you're staying?"

"If you want me to." He held his breath, waiting for her answer. Leaving now would be sheer torture, but if he stayed, it had to be her choice.

She hesitated a moment, then lowered her eyes and whispered, "Yes, I want that very much."

He exhaled forcefully, a little giddy with relief. "I guess you didn't intend to sleep much tonight, anyway, right?"

She gave him the wide-eyed look that he'd come to cherish. "I . . . guess not."

He shifted to his side, tumbling her gently to the cushiony surface of the quilt. "Good. Now, if you'll tell me where I can find some extra blankets, I'll make things a little more comfortable for us."

She tried to get up to help, but he wouldn't allow it. When he'd fashioned a cozy nest for them from quilts and blankets, he drew her close once more and indulged himself in learning the glorious perfection of her body. More quickly than he expected, the passion flamed again. But this time, when he tried to pull her atop him, she resisted.

"Max." Her voice was a soft whisper as she drew him down to lie over her. "I think I'd like to try it this way." Her soft thighs parted, inviting him, and his heart contracted at the inherent trust in that simple act.

I love you, Liana. He couldn't be sure if he'd said the words or merely thought them, as he eased into her snug, welcoming heat. But the truth of them seared his soul. He loved her. What he felt went beyond superficial sexual fascination. He loved her courage and her resourcefulness, even her loyalty to her father. But most of all, he loved her for the trust she'd shown in him by giving herself so totally.

In honor of that trust, he held back a little, allowing her time to become accustomed to the weight of his body. It wasn't easy for her at first. He could feel her hesitancy, as he sank into her fully. But at last, she accepted him completely, her arms and slender legs drawing him ever nearer. They seemed to reach new heights, their second time together. Afterward he realized that, for him, the added dimension was love. The catch was, he couldn't tell her.

Watching her doze lightly in the golden glow of firelight, he let the anguish of that thought settle in. There were too many things unresolved between them—the major one being her father's ranch. If that turned out the way he expected, she might resent him so much, she might never be able to return his love. A pain more devastating than anything he'd ever known lanced through him. He'd lost her once. He didn't think he could bear to lose her again.

Anxious to deny the possibility, he pulled her tightly into his embrace, and in so doing bumped the nesting box. The baby owl let out a protesting squeak, and Max reluctantly released Liana to go quiet it.

"Max?" She rose up on one elbow to peer at him, her gaze flickering over his nakedness. The blanket they'd been sharing slipped off of her shoulder and she pulled it back up self-consciously.

"It's all right, love." Could she hear the new emotion behind that endearment? "Your star boarder just got a little restless."

She frowned anxiously. "Will he be okay? I mean, what if his parents won't take him back?"

"Don't worry. They'll welcome him with open, er, wings. Barn owls are known for their loyalty."

She sat up, hugging the blanket to her breasts with a modesty that charmed him. "You're beginning to sound like an authority on them."

He shrugged. "I did some research when I put up the nesting boxes. I learned a lot from the Project Wildlife people. They gave me a hand a couple of times with injured and orphaned birds."

The owlet had quieted, so he moved back to Liana's side and rejoined her under the blanket. "The more I learn about them, the more I like them." He looked straight into her eyes before adding, "They mate for life, you know—" An idea he found enormously appealing as he gazed at her.

A lovely rose color suffused her cheeks. "Is that unusual?"

"Yes. In raptors *and* in homo sapiens, these days." He traced the satin softness of her mouth with the tip of his finger. Her lips were slightly swollen from his kisses, and it made him want to kiss her again. "When I marry, it'll be a lifetime commitment." Leaning over, he briefly touched his mouth to hers, but when he started to move closer, she forestalled him with a hand on his chest.

"Is that how you felt about the girl you were supposed to marry in France?"

Was that jealousy he saw in her eyes? If so, there was hope for them. "So, you know about that."

"Not really. Sybille just told me a little bit about it." She stopped suddenly and bit her lip.

The idea that Sybille had been gossiping about his personal affairs caused him to frown. "What, exactly, did she say?"

Liana's gaze slipped sideways to the fire. "She said the girl backed out because she couldn't stand the competition."

"And you believe that?"

She faced him a little defiantly. "I don't know what to think. You're entirely different than I expected, and after what we just did together, I'm not sure I can trust my judgment anymore."

He sighed and lay down beside her on his back, his gaze fixed on the ceiling. "Then listen to the truth. Annette didn't back out because she thought there were other women." He'd overcome the bitterness years ago, but he couldn't suppress a note of irony in his voice as he went on. "When my father died and I had to come home to run the winery, she decided she didn't love me enough to leave her family and friends. So she married a local man. The last I heard, they had six kids and were working on the seventh."

"She broke your heart," Liana whispered wonderingly.

"Yeah, but I got over it. However, there's one heartbreak I never did forget."

He sensed her hesitation to probe further, but evidently her curiosity was stronger. "Who was she?"

Shifting to his side, he pulled her down to face him. "You, love."

Her straight dark eyebrows arched up in surprise. "When did this amazing event supposedly happen?"

"Fourteen years ago."

She lightly thumped his chest with her fist. "You've got the facts twisted around. I was the one whose heart was broken, remember? You rejected me because you thought I was too young."

He gently touched his nose to hers. "And every time you looked at me with those tragic eyes of yours, it broke my heart. It took me a long time to forget that look."

"But you did forget," she said, retreating a bit from his nuzzling.

"I thought I had—" He pressed his hand on the small of her back to bring their naked bodies into exquisite contact. "Until the day you returned to the valley."

"Max..." Her voice trailed off in a soft gasp as he slid down to bury his face in the lush curve of her bosom.

"You are so lovely here." He opened his mouth over her tender flesh. "You taste like honey and cream, and I'm developing a voracious appetite for that combination."

She laughed unevenly. "Sounds dangerous. Maybe I should go get you something to eat."

"Maybe later. I have everything I need right now, love." Now and forever, if she'd have him. He wanted to tell her that, but since he couldn't yet, he settled for showing her his adoration the only other way possible at the moment.

This time her passion flared like a spark on dry kindling, but he took his time, using his fingertips and his tongue to learn the most intimate secrets of her body. He drew her higher and higher until she was trembling and calling his name. When he plunged deep inside her at last, the incandescent explosion came almost immediately.

Afterward, as she slumbered, exhausted, in his arms, he caught himself wondering how in the world he'd go on with life if he lost her again.

LIANA AWAKENED TO THE owlet's noisy demands for food, and instantly realized she was alone beneath the blanket. Gray light seeped through the coarse weave of the living-room draperies, telling her that morning had arrived. When she listened closely, she realized the rain had stopped. But where was Max? Memories of the night before cascaded over her, bringing a jumble of emotions she couldn't begin to sort out, except for a soul-wrenching sense of desolation. After what they'd shared, could he have left without even saying goodbye?

"Good morning." His deep voice jolted her out of her morose thoughts. She whipped her head around and found him standing in the doorway of the kitchen wearing only his dark slacks and holding a small bowl in his hand. His hair was rumpled from sleep and a shadow of beard darkened his lower face, but to her anxious eyes he was the most beautiful male she'd ever seen.

Was she falling in love with the man? Her stomach tightened convulsively at the thought. No, that couldn't be right. Being swept away by passion was one thing, but there was still the matter of her loyalty to her father and his land. How could she love a man who stood so completely in the way of her father's happiness?

"I . . . I thought you'd left." She averted her eyes, confused by the emotions roiling inside of her.

He padded across the wooden floor on bare feet, and knelt on the quilt to give her a warm, lingering kiss. "Not yet. Although I'll have to get back to my place before too long and check for storm damage." He set the bowl aside and cupped her face with both hands. "How are you, this morning? It occurred to me when I woke up that we may have overdone things last night."

She stretched experimentally and winced. Her body ached in places she normally didn't think about, but she certainly wasn't prepared to discuss that. "I'm fine."

"Sure, you are," he said teasingly. "I think I'd better go feed our greedy raptor. If I don't, I might be tempted to find out if you're telling the truth." He moved over to the nesting box and took a small strip of raw chicken from the bowl to offer to the owlet. "I'd like to get his home reestablished as soon as possible. He needs to get back on his regular diet."

That meant Max would be leaving soon, she thought, fighting another wave of dejection. "Don't you want some breakfast first? I have eggs, bacon, whatever you'd like."

He sent her one of his most sexy smiles. "What I'd like, I can't have." He nodded toward the little pile of discarded wrappers on the floor. "We used the last of those in the early hours of the morning."

She felt herself blushing. "Oh."

He chuckled softly. "But I'll settle for coffee."

Firmly gathering the blanket around her, she snatched up her scattered clothing and rose to leave. "I'll go start the coffee and get dressed." She hurried out of the room, nearly tripping on the blanket.

A while later, as she dressed in jeans and a sweater, she tried to sort out her emotions. Preoccupied with her inner struggle, she descended the stairs and entered the living room. But she paused warily when she saw Max. He was standing by her father's desk with a sheaf of papers in his hand. "What are you doing?"

He started guiltily, then gave her an uneasy smile. "I'm sorry. These fell on the floor when I was folding the quilt, and I started reading them before I realized what they were." He replaced the papers on the desk and came toward her. "But I'm impressed with what I saw. It's too bad we're not on the same side. Together we could achieve national distribution for Valentin Winery in no time."

Her wariness burgeoned into full-blown suspicion. He'd read her proposal for the bank loan? She moved to put the couch between them. "But that can't possibly happen unless I don't succeed in helping my father keep the property, can it? And it would be to your advantage to know what I intend to propose, wouldn't it?"

All of a sudden the full impact of what she'd allowed to happen struck her: she'd slept with the enemy. On the heels of that awful thought came another, borne of the terrible sense of betrayal looming in her heart. "Or maybe you think that just because I let you make love to me, I'll be willing to betray my father?"

Max's expression darkened. "Now, just a minute. You're jumping to conclusions, here. And they're wrong—dead wrong."

"That's what you say. But I can't help but wonder if I'm being beguiled just like everyone else that crosses your path—horses and owls included. If so, you'd be the last to admit it."

Max started to say something, then checked himself and ran a hand over his face, visibly controlling his temper. "Look, honey, I think I know where this is coming from. You're feeling a little uncertain this morning, and I can understand that. What we had last night was enough to shake anyone. But that doesn't give you the right to make wild accusations about my intentions."

"Making love to me doesn't give you the right to go spying through my business papers," she countered.

"I was not spying," he said defensively.

She made a soft sound of disbelief. "I think you'd better leave."

His mouth tightened, but then he nodded curtly. "I think you're right. There's no point in trying to reason with you right now. You're so scared of your own feelings you can't see the truth." He stalked over to the nesting box and picked it up. "I'll call you later, and we'll see if we can work this out."

"Don't bother. As long as the issue of my dad's land stands between us, I don't think it's a good idea for us to be, uh, seeing each other."

He crossed the room and stopped in front of her, the box balanced in the crook of his arm. As she stared at

him defiantly, he again made an obvious effort to rein
in his emotions. "I don't think you mean that—not after the way you gave yourself to me last night."

She closed her eyes briefly, steeling herself against the
wanton images he'd called forth. "I wasn't thinking
clearly then. I am now."

"Are you?" He sighed in frustration. "All right, then.
I'll give you a few days to think things over, before I
call." He strode toward the kitchen, then paused in the
doorway and faced her one last time. "Keep this in mind
while you're thinking, though. You weren't the only one
swept away last night, love. You're the best thing that's
happened to me in a long time, and I'm not going to give
that up without a fight."

BY THE TIME MAX GOT back home that night, he was
cold, muddy and exhausted. He'd managed to replace
the nesting box, with a little help from the utility crew
that was repairing the power lines. Then he'd spent the
balance of the day checking the vineyards for damage.
Fortunately, there hadn't been any, but that hadn't lifted
his spirits much. In spite of all the things he had to keep
his mind occupied, his thoughts kept revolving around
one topic: Liana.

Now all he wanted was a hot shower, clean clothes
and some time to think of a solution. His mood
dropped significantly when he entered the back door
to his kitchen and found Sybille sitting at the small
breakfast table waiting for him. The kitchen had been
his grandmother's haven, and he'd faithfully restored
the antique cabinets to the sunny yellow she'd loved.

Having Sybille there seemed to dim the room's bright cheerfulness.

"You look like a mud wrestler," she pronounced, wrinkling her nose in distaste.

He gave her a dark look. "I feel like one. What are you doing here?"

"I just came to see if you were all right." She paused meaningfully. "You were gone all night. I was concerned."

He bent and pulled off his mud-caked boots. "I thought the agreement was you don't question my activities, and I don't notice who's sneaking in and out of the big house at odd hours." He didn't add particulars—like Jeff Moser's name—but they both knew who he was talking about.

She went rigid. "I'm not questioning you. I'm just worried that you might be overextending yourself. You seem distracted lately, and you've been spending more and more time at the Castillo place." Sybille's mouth tightened in a travesty of a smile. "If you're not careful, she'll have you helping her buy out that lease."

At another time he might've held on to his temper, but after the day he'd had, he didn't feel like suffering Sybille's meddling in silence. "What if I did decide to help her? It's my land, isn't it? If I wanted to *give* it to her, I could."

A muscle in Sybille's jaw twitched, and her eyes widened in horror. "You would do that?"

"Not would, could." Leaving his boots on the porch, he stepped inside and approached her, arms folded over his chest. "The point is, the choice is mine."

She got up, gesturing angrily. "I'm only thinking of what's best for the business, and reclaiming that property is the only way we can afford to expand right now. How can you think of letting it go to a crazy old man who can't even manage the place?"

"Calm down, will you? I'm not letting anything go yet." He deliberately turned his back on her and went to the sink for a glass of water. To his irritation, Sybille stomped after him.

"Calm down? How can I calm down when there's a good possibility Liana might manage to find the money to buy out the lease. Jeff says she's fixing up the place and looking for more horses to board."

Max lowered the glass he'd been drinking from and scrutinized her suspiciously. "Jeff? How does he know all this?"

Her gaze darted away, and she ran a fingernail along the white-tiled countertop. "He's been doing some work for her."

"Whose idea was that?"

Her shoulders jerked in a little shrug. "His, I suppose. He offered to fix that old wreck her father drives."

"Then he comes over here and reports everything he's found out." Max didn't try to hide the disdain he felt. Someone ought to tell Jeff Moser just how thoroughly he was being used. But then something clicked in Max's brain.

"Wait a minute," he said, pinning Sybille with a glance. "Arlie Moser was Jeff's cousin, wasn't he? Why would Jeff want to work for the Castillos when Frank's made no secret of his hatred for Mosers?"

"How should I know?" She pushed away from the counter and went to the back door.

Max's suspicions deepened. "You'd better not be using him to spy on Liana."

She spun around indignantly. "You're always so quick to accuse, aren't you? But you never seem to notice all I've done to help build this place." To his amazement there were tears in her eyes and she suddenly looked distraught.

Trust Sybille to always consider herself the wronged party, he thought, sighing in annoyance. Yet, he had to admit she had been a good worker, in spite of her tendency to butt in where she wasn't wanted. "Look, I do appreciate all you've done around here. But I won't allow anyone to add to Liana's troubles right now. She has more than enough."

Sybille's distress deepened. "Now you're protecting her? It's worse than I thought, then. You're falling in love with her."

Max frowned. He didn't want that getting around—especially when he couldn't tell Liana yet. "I don't fall in love, remember?"

"So you say. But if you're not careful, you're liable to end up like my Rennie." With that oblique warning she left, slamming the door behind her.

9

A SMALL CLOUD OF GLOOM hovered threateningly over Liana as she entered the ranch's plain but comfortingly familiar kitchen. Ever since the night of the storm, she'd been hard-pressed to maintain an optimistic view on anything. The main cause was the azure-eyed specter who'd been haunting her thoughts and dreams incessantly for the past three days. No matter how many times she told herself to stop thinking about him, he just wouldn't go away.

She sighed wearily and slipped her aching feet out of the high-heeled pumps she'd worn to make the rounds of the local financial institutions. That grueling exercise had taken up most of the day, and now that she was back home, she couldn't wait to get into more comfortable clothes.

Upstairs in her bedroom, she quickly donned jeans and a cotton sweater. As she tugged on a pair of tennis shoes, there was a knock on the door. Everything inside her froze. *Max?* He'd said he'd be back to talk things out with her, and she'd been half expecting him to show up ever since. Now her heart began an undisciplined dance of anticipation, despite the fact that she was determined that he wouldn't beguile her again.

Though dreading the ordeal of facing him, she went to answer the door. But when she opened it, Sybille was waiting for her on the front stoop. Stunned, Liana barely managed a hello.

"I was passing by, and thought I'd stop in to see how you were doing," Sybille said. Something about her smile made Liana feel uneasy.

"I'm . . . uh . . . wonderful." She hesitated, wondering whether or not she should invite the woman in.

"I heard that your power was out during the storm, as was ours," Sybille went on smoothly. "I hope you had everything you needed."

Talk about an understatement! Liana thought, as her mind replayed selected erotic images for the thousandth time. Concerned that Sybille might somehow sense the subject of her thoughts, Liana said coolly, "Storms don't bother me. We have lots of them in Oregon."

"Oh? When Max didn't come home the other night, I thought perhaps he'd spent the night here because you were afraid to be alone."

Liana felt herself blushing at the woman's implication, but she also experienced a flash of outrage. "I don't think that's your—" she choked on the word *affair* and substituted "—business."

Guilt flickered briefly in Sybille's eyes, but then she leaned forward with what appeared to be real concern. "Forgive me. I know I shouldn't interfere, but I feel someone should warn you. Especially considering all you stand to lose. Max can be very . . . charming when he wants something, but he told me himself just the other day that he never falls in love. Once he gets what he's after, you'll cease to exist for him. I've seen it happen more times than I care to say."

The fact that she'd thought the same thing only increased Liana's chagrin. It was bad enough to suspect she'd been duped by Max, but to have someone else think it—particularly Sybille—was intolerable.

"Have you considered the possibility that the situation is reversed this time?" She knew there wasn't any possibility of that being the case, but she felt good just saying it. Sybille looked slightly taken aback, which made Liana feel even better.

"Furthermore, it'll take a lot more than charm to keep me from helping my father. I'm expecting a call soon from one of the local banks. They were very enthusiastic about my loan application." Not exactly the truth, but she knew that Sybille would probably report every word back to Max, and the idea of shaking his confidence was too tempting to resist.

An indefinable emotion darkened Sybille's eyes. "I can see we may have underestimated you. Still, I felt it was my duty to warn you about Max. Since I've done that, I'll leave." She turned and started down the porch steps.

"I appreciate the gesture," Liana said, lying through her teeth.

Sybille glanced back at her. "It was nothing. Just be careful who you trust from now on."

Present company included? Liana wondered, as she watched the older woman start off toward the Valentin property.

THE NEXT MORNING LIANA was heading for the stable when Jeff Moser arrived on his bike. As it frequently did in the valley, the weather had turned unseasonably warm, and his pale hair clung to his forehead in damp spikes.

"The parts for the truck came in." He indicated the large backpack he wore with a jerk of his thumb. "So I thought I'd get started, if it's all right with you."

Liana nodded. "The sooner the better. I'll be in the stable if you need anything." She continued on her way, feeling slightly more optimistic. If she had the truck to drive, she could return Max's car.

At noon, Jeff appeared to announce it was time for him to leave for his other job. Liana had been preparing to clean Sonny's stall, but she paused.

"I want you to know how much I appreciate your work on Dad's truck. It probably would have cost me a lot more to have it fixed in a shop." She gave him a friendly grin. "I admit I was a little suspicious when you asked for the job. I might not have hired you if Sybille hadn't recommended you so highly. Now I'm glad I did."

To her amazement, her admission seemed to thoroughly disconcert him. He turned away, hands shoved in his pockets, and stammered out a promise to return the next day.

His behavior struck Liana as odd, but she quickly forgot about it as she opened the outer door of Sonny's stall, then went back inside to shoo him into the adjoining paddock. She worked steadily, having become reaccustomed to physical labor. And except for the occasional meow from one of the stable cats, silence reigned. She was just arranging a fresh layer of straw when she thought she heard something outside. Had Jeff returned for some reason?

A sharp crack rent the air, followed by Sonny's indignant whinny. Then came the thunder of his hooves as he charged into the stall, nearly crushing her against the rear wall. She dropped the pitchfork she'd been using and dodged to the side, panic exploding within her chest. Desperately she gauged the distance to the open door, but as she did so it slammed shut, as if propelled from outside.

Sonny screamed and reared, crashing his hooves against the side of the stall. Liana pressed herself flat against the opposite wall, trying hard not to scream herself. "Easy, boy, easy," she said, her voice shaking. She ducked sideways just as the horse angrily kicked the wall behind him, narrowly missing her. He rolled his eyes wildly—the whites stark against his black face—and he lunged sideways, nearly pinning her to the side of the stall.

Realizing there was only one avenue of escape, she turned and grabbed the top of the stall's inner door, hoisting herself up until she could get one leg over. Behind her she could hear Sonny thrashing around, and she sensed his wicked yellow teeth reaching for her as she hurled herself over the side of the stall. When she landed, her knees buckled and a silent scream reverberated in her head.

Then she screamed aloud as two hands clamped on her waist from behind. She was spun around and found herself staring into Max's worried face.

"Liana? Take it easy, it's only me. What the heck's going on here?"

She tried to answer him, but the gasping breaths she'd been taking suddenly erupted into heavy sobs. The next thing she knew, she was being drawn into his warm, strong embrace. Even though a tiny segment of her mind cried out a protest, she needed reassurance too much to resist.

He held her, murmuring words of comfort as his hands smoothed over her back. Gradually her shudders of relief quieted, but in their place came more distressing sensations. She became aware of his hard, vital body pressing against hers, and memories of their night together flared and caught like wildfire within her. She made a soft sound—half denial, half assent—and then he shifted her in his arms and she felt the soul-stirring pressure of his lips against hers. But even as the magic began to swirl through her again, a warning sounded in her mind: she couldn't let him do this, not again. With an anguished cry, she shoved away from him and backed up a few feet. "That wasn't fair. I told you there couldn't be anything more between us."

He sighed in frustration. "Hey, I lost my head. That seems to happen every time I hold you." His eyes shifted to Sonny. "What's going on? I heard Sonny carrying on. Then I saw you come vaulting out of his stall. What were you doing in there? You know he's skittish around you."

"It wasn't intentional, believe me." She sat down on an overturned bucket so he wouldn't see how much that one kiss had shaken her. Meanwhile, Sonny had calmed down completely and was whickering softly at Max over the stall's door.

The traitor! She glared at the horse resentfully. "I'd put him outside in the paddock and was cleaning his stall when something spooked him and he came charging back inside. Then the door slammed shut behind him, and I was trapped." She shuddered, remembering. "I haven't been that scared in a long time."

"You could've been killed." Emotion roughened Max's voice, and when she glanced at him he looked as shaken as she felt. "Do you have any idea what might've caused him to do that?"

She shook her head. "I heard a sharp cracking noise, but I don't know what it was. Did you see anything unusual outside?"

"Nothing. But then, I walked over from the vineyards, so I couldn't see the paddock or the outer door to Sonny's stall as I approached. I think I'll go look around out there."

"You don't have to do that."

He reproached her with a look. "Yes, I do. If nothing else, for my own peace of mind."

She followed him outside, and they combed the area for clues. But they found nothing that could explain the incident.

"Maybe it was a car backfiring," Max suggested at last. He swung the paddock gate shut and secured it.

Liana looked down the long drive leading to the main road. "I don't think so. It sounded more like someone cracking a whip."

Concern darkened Max's eyes. "Then you think someone deliberately frightened Sonny?"

The idea astounded her. "Like who? You said you didn't see anyone as you walked over here. And I haven't seen anyone since Jeff left around noon."

Max's gaze sharpened. "The Moser kid was here today?"

"He's hardly a kid, but yes. He's fixing my dad's truck."

"Do you think that's wise, considering the bad feelings between his family and your father? What if he's harboring a secret grudge against you?"

She exhaled impatiently. "Now you sound just like my father. Jeff doesn't buy into any of that animosity, and he claims his family has all but forgotten it." Of course, there had been that disturbing conversation with his sister, when she mentioned his despondency over his cousin's death. But he'd probably gotten over that, years ago.

"Aside from that," she said aloud, "there isn't any evidence that the incident with Sonny was more than an accident. As for my father's feelings, Jeff said he'd be finished by the end of the week, and Dad won't be coming home till the following Friday, so they probably won't even see each other."

"I still think you should be careful around Jeff. Sybille's had him under her spell for some time—and I'm not talking about a platonic relationship."

Liana gaped at him in shock. "But she's old enough—"

"To be his mother," Max put in, looking disgusted. "I can't say that I approve of the relationship, but she and I have an agreement about not interfering in each other's lives, so I stay out of it."

Too bad Sybille doesn't feel obligated to hold up her side of the bargain, Liana thought.

Max leaned back against the paddock gate and gave her a penetrating look. "Now, about us."

A quiver of anxiety ran down her spine. "That's a closed subject."

"I'm opening it again. And I'm not leaving until I make you see that what happened between us has nothing to do with that lease. I would never do anything to sabotage your efforts on your father's behalf, and I think it was unfair of you to assume I would. Granted, if you managed to get a bank loan and buy out, it'd mess up my plans, but it wouldn't change the way I feel about you."

He looked so sincere, his deep blue gaze never leaving her face, as he stood with the afternoon breeze ruffling his ebony hair. She caught herself wanting to believe him, in spite of the doubts tormenting her heart. Closing her eyes, she tried to think rationally, but a picture of his compelling face remained in her mind's eye like the afterimage left by a flash camera.

"Liana," he said with sudden urgency. "Look at me. Can't you see that this is real?"

She opened her eyes, but the rush of emotion she felt at seeing him again, only increased her confusion. How could she know what was real, and what was not, when just the sight of him made her pulse accelerate?

"Trust isn't that easy for me," she whispered. "You're asking too much, Max."

He looked down at the toes of his boots for several moments, and she saw the muscles of his jaw tighten. When he looked up again, impatience flashed in his eyes. "Maybe I am. But a relationship without trust is like a grapevine without good rootstock. When the hard times come, it withers and dies."

Her heart skipped a beat. He sounded as if he were talking about something permanent. "We don't have a relationship."

That seemed to irritate him even more. "We have the beginnings of one, and we could have more if you had a little faith in me. I've done everything I can to earn your trust, but I've almost decided I'm wasting my time." He stepped away from the gate, his expression grim. "You can't keep pushing a man away and expect him to keep coming back for more. The choice is yours, Liana. Think about it."

Thoroughly nonplused by his challenge, Liana stood speechless as he walked off toward his vineyard. She hadn't even considered the possibility of a relationship with another man since John's death. In her estimation, the sexual demands far outweighed the benefits.

At least they had until she'd rediscovered Max Valentin.

A delicate shudder ran through her—a sensual aftershock from that night of passionate abandon. It wasn't the first reverberation she'd felt, but this one was much stronger. Over the next few days, the sensation recurred each time she remembered his words, adding to the emotional battle raging inside her. She might have thought of nothing else, if the daily routine around the ranch hadn't kept her so busy.

JEFF SHOWED UP IN THE morning ready for work, and although he continued to act uneasy around her, she couldn't believe it was anything more than simple bashfulness. When she casually asked him if he'd returned to the ranch at any time the previous afternoon, he'd responded negatively and without hesitation.

As he'd promised, the truck was running by Friday, but when she asked him about his offer to stay on and do some trash hauling, he flushed and looked apologetic.

"I know I said I'd do that, but . . . Well, something's come up, and I'll be leaving town sooner than I thought."

"Has your date to report to boot camp changed?"

Jeff's freckled face turned scarlet. "Nah. Things have just been getting complicated around here, and I decided it was time to make a clean break."

Liana remembered what Max had said about Sybille's involvement with Jeff, and decided not to pursue the subject. Instead, she paid him for his work and wished him well, adding, "If you change your mind, my offer stands."

SHE BROUGHT HER FATHER home the last Friday in May, with a heavy cast on his leg and crutches, which he despised. Because the daytime temperatures had continued to soar, he was hot and uncomfortable by the time they got inside the house.

"Know what I could use?" He eased down on the couch and let Liana hoist the cast up on it. "Some of my honey wine. It's the only thing that hospital kitchen couldn't provide."

She hesitated. Wine at two o'clock in the afternoon? Well, it was probably no worse than the painkillers the doctor had prescribed. Since her father had refused to take any more of the pills, perhaps a little wine wouldn't hurt. When she brought a small glassful to him, he thanked her with a tired smile.

She wasn't too happy when he insisted on having another glass with dinner and a third afterward, but he wouldn't take no for an answer. When he woke at midnight complaining of stomach pains, she suspected the wine instantly.

"Dad, didn't you tell me you had this kind of distress before you went into the hospital?" She sat on the edge of his bed, and touched his forehead to check for signs of fever. His skin felt dry and not overly warm.

He winced and rubbed his stomach. "Yeah, but that was my lousy cooking."

She frowned. "Do you think it might have been something you ate? I haven't felt any bad effects from our dinner and we had the same thing—except for your wine."

He shook his head. "I can't believe there could be anything wrong with my wine. I've been making the stuff ever since you moved to Oregon, and this stomach trouble only started a couple of years ago." His expression darkened suddenly. "Unless someone's been trying to poison me. It'd certainly suit Valentin's plans if I wasn't around to buy out that lease."

From the depths of her soul a protest welled up, surprising in its intensity. Max wasn't capable of doing anything like that. With sudden, dismaying acuity, she also realized he would never sabotage her efforts to get a bank loan. Her suspicions had been just as unfair as her father's. Maybe more so, since she'd actually voiced her distrust to Max. What a nasty blow that must have been after the breathtaking intimacy they'd shared the night before. Guilt stung her conscience.

Her father grunted softly, pulling her from her musings. "I know you think I've been imagining things, but I'm telling you, someone has been out to get me. The most likely suspect is Valentin."

Knowing she couldn't leap to Max's defense without arousing her father's suspicions, she tried another tack. "I simply think you're overreacting about the wine. If there is anything wrong with it, I have a hunch it'll be something straightforward, like an allergic reaction, or contamination during the fermenting or bottling process. Still, I think we should have it checked. In the meantime, you're not getting any more."

When she repeated her suspicions to her father's doctor the next morning, he suggested the problem was most likely an allergic reaction, rather than toxicity in the wine. But he agreed to have the wine analyzed by a friend who worked in a lab.

Two days later, the doctor called back. "The wine was toxic, all right," he announced abruptly. "My friend couldn't be sure whether the toxicity came from one of the original ingredients or from something added to the wine after it was made. But his gut feeling leaned toward the latter." He laughed gruffly. "Your father doesn't have any enemies, does he?"

A tendril of fear suddenly curled around her heart. "Are you suggesting someone deliberately poisoned the wine?"

"Good Lord, no! I was just joking. The source of the problem is probably something as simple as improperly sterilized equipment." In spite of his assurances, a lingering sense of disquiet haunted Liana for the rest of the day.

The following morning her mood deepened to gloom when two of the banks she'd approached called in succession to turn down her father's loan application. When yet another bank's loan officer called the next afternoon, she wasn't too surprised when he apologetically advised her that her request had been denied there, also.

"That leaves only one prospect," she told her father, as they sat across from each other at dinner that evening. "And they were the least enthusiastic when I approached them." Even though she hated giving him bad news while he was still convalescing, the time had come for discussing backup plans. She'd gently broached the subject several times before, but he'd always side-stepped it.

Now, he paused with a forkful of salad halfway to his mouth and gave her a slightly belligerent look. "There are other banks in this county."

She stifled a sigh and toyed with the assortment of greens and fresh vegetables on her plate. The warm weather had made a dinner salad sound tempting, but now she felt her appetite vanishing.

"I don't think approaching them will help," she said reluctantly. "Not with money as tight as it is right now. I was counting on a little small-town loyalty to overcome the odds against us. But even the bank you've dealt with for years couldn't give an approval, based on your current financial status."

He set the fork down without tasting the salad, his weathered features tensing. "Does that mean I'm finished?"

The utter despair in his voice hit her like a punch in the stomach, but she tried to maintain a calm front. "No. What it means is, we should be thinking of a contingency plan, in case you can't stay here."

A slow, weary breath escaped him, and he seemed to sag and age right before her eyes. "If I lose this place, it won't matter much where I go." He ran a gnarled hand through his silver hair. "Funny, I guess I never really believed Valentin could drive me out."

The blatant untruthfulness of his assertion was too much for Liana to let pass unchallenged. She'd tried to keep her feelings about Max to herself, but the time had come for honesty. "He didn't drive you out, Dad," she said quietly. "From what I can see, he's bent over backward to give you a chance to save this place. He could've thrown you out months ago when you got behind in your lease payments. But instead, he gave you another chance . . . and another."

"You sound as if you're on his side." The sharp note of hurt in his voice wounded her as much as the accusation. The fact that he was partly right didn't dull the pain at all.

"Why do I have to choose sides?" she demanded, tears stinging her eyes. Distressed by the look of betrayal on his face, she got up and took her plate to the sink.

"What's he done to you?" her father demanded with unexpected insight. "You didn't fall for that infamous charm of his, did you? I warned you about his reputation as a ladies' man."

She opened her mouth to fling back an impulsive defense, then checked herself. At twenty-eight, she shouldn't have to justify her private life to her father. Just the same, it hurt to have her integrity questioned. "I don't think that's the issue here," she said, trying to keep her voice even. "I'm doing everything in my power to save this place for you. I think it's really unfair of you to suggest that anyone could persuade me to give anything less than my best effort."

Her father swore—a vice he rarely gave in to. "I didn't mean to imply you hadn't. You've done wonders around here. Far more than I intended for you to do. I just hate to hear you defending the man who's going to take it all away from me."

The weeks of exhausting labor and emotional turmoil had taken their toll on Liana, and she suddenly found his self-delusion was more than she could bear. The taut rein she'd been holding on her temper snapped. "How can you say he's taking it away from you, when you're the one who let the place slip into financial ruin?" She regretted the words instantly, but there was no way to retrieve them.

Her father twisted abruptly in his chair, turning away from her. "I guess I deserved that," he said heavily. He attempted to get up, struggling clumsily with the crutches.

"Dad, wait. Let me—" She rushed to help him, but he waved her away.

"I want to be alone for a while," he announced when he'd managed to stand. "I'll be in my room."

Her heart aching, she watched him hobble away, his head held high with a remnant of dignity. Automatically, she washed the dishes and put the kitchen in order, but the turmoil within her grew stronger and stronger, demanding a more physical outlet.

Immediately, the pond came to mind. She hadn't been there since that first morning after her arrival, and a swim would feel heavenly after the day's heat.

By the time she reached the water's edge, the moon had risen like a pale porcelain saucer on the darkening horizon. The sky was clear, except for the sparkling light of a million stars and a slight encroachment of clouds over the mountains to the west. She tossed her towel onto a nearby bush, shimmied out of her shorts and waded into the cool water wearing only a yellow tank top and high-cut white panties. To keep her hair out of her eyes, she'd secured it high on her head in a ponytail.

The water lapped against her warm skin like cool silk. As soon as she was in deep enough to swim, she launched herself into a series of fast laps across the deepest portion of the pond. The exertion worked like magic on her overwrought nerves, and when she stopped to catch her breath, she felt better than she had in a long time. She inhaled deeply, savoring the fresh verdant scent of new grass and wildflowers, gifts from the recent storm.

As always, just thinking of that night brought a cascade of memories. But this time, instead of fighting them, she closed her eyes and let the images come. The water gently supported her as she floated on her back, and she felt as if she could drift forever.

"Would you look at this? A rare, fresh-water mermaid."

Startled, she floundered to her feet in the waist-deep water and saw Max standing at the water's edge. "What are you doing here? How did you get there without me hearing you?"

He swung a hand in the direction of his property. "I walked, and I didn't make any attempt to be quiet about it. You must have been deep in some dream, if you didn't

hear me. As for my reason for being here..." He smiled
and began to unbutton his blue-and-white striped shirt.

Her heart did a crazy little leap. "Don't you dare."

His grin broadened. "Why not? I swim here quite often. Especially when a certain lady I know gets me all
heated up, and I can't do anything about it." He slipped
the shirt off and hung it on a low-hanging branch.

When his hands moved to his belt buckle she
squawked, "I thought you'd decided I was a waste of
your time."

"Not quite. Seeing you like this makes me want to
give you another chance." He began to ease his snug
jeans down, and the determined glint in his eyes made
her panic. She struck out for the opposite shore as fast
as she could swim. She'd nearly reached her destination when two strong hands gripped her waist, pulling
her back to deeper water.

"You didn't have a chance, little mermaid," he said,
laughing. "I told you I swim here often." His arms
wrapped around her, thwarting the frantic thrashing
of her arms. The level of the water came to just below
her breasts, but she couldn't seem to find her footing.

She twisted in an effort to get away, and found herself confronted with the mesmerizing face that had been
haunting her dreams. His black hair was wet and
slicked back and droplets of water clung to his mar-
velous features like liquid diamonds. All thoughts of
escape vanished, as exhilaration shot through her like
a comet. Against all reason, she felt as if she'd just discovered the answer to all her problems.

"Max," she whispered, her breath stalling in her throat.

Desire deepened the color of his eyes until they almost turned black. "Oh, love, you know what it does to me when you say my name like that." His warm wet mouth found hers. All else faded to insignificance. This time there was no subtlety in his kiss—only a raw demand for what she'd given so completely once before. And she gave it again, opening her mouth to his delicious invasion, wrapping her arms around his shoulders until her breasts were pressed against his hard chest. She returned his kisses ravenously, until they both had to stop to breathe.

"I didn't expect such a warm welcome." A teasing light twinkled in his eyes. "I hope it's because you've been thinking of me."

"I may have, once or twice." She gasped as his teeth captured her earlobe in a gentle reprimand. "Maybe three times."

"I can't stop thinking about you," he murmured. "Day and night. I have trouble concentrating on my work, and I can't sleep without dreaming about you."

She drew a shaky breath. "Sounds serious."

He tilted her head up and looked directly into her eyes. "I am serious. More serious than you know. If you weren't so worried about my having nefarious plans to take your father's land, I could show you."

She ducked her head, remembering how she'd mistrusted him. "I need to apologize to you for that. I finally realized how wrong I was about you. Although, I guess that's a moot point, now."

His hands tightened on her shoulders. "Why? What's happened?"

Some of her earlier distress came creeping back, like the thick clouds she could see rolling in from the western horizon. "Almost all of the banks have turned us down. At this rate, we won't be able to buy out the lease."

He gripped her harder. "Then what will you do?"

"I don't know. I've tried to discuss it with my father, but we're getting nowhere." She gestured helplessly. "He won't even consider moving to Oregon with me."

Max frowned and gave her a gentle shake. "I don't want that, either. In fact, if I didn't need the land myself, I'd let you and your father continue using it on the condition that you didn't leave."

His admission thrilled her, even though it was hopeless. "He'd never accept charity. You should know that. And without the ranch, there really isn't any reason for me to stay."

"What about this one?" he demanded. His mouth captured hers with a sudden fierce need that made her pulse leap. His hands roved urgently over her back, then slid down to mold the curve of her bottom, hauling her against the heat of his body. "You can't leave, Liana," he said, his voice raspy with need. "Not now. There has to be another way."

She moaned as his palms cupped her breasts through the soaked material of her tank top, generating an effervescent heat that radiated throughout her body.

"I don't want to leave." The admission slipped from her almost before she knew it herself. With it came the realization that, regardless of what happened next, she loved Max Valentin.

He angled back to study her face, a mix of hope and longing in his expression. "Then we'll work it out somehow." Bending his head, he charted the delicate curve of her shoulder with his mouth. "Do you know what I saw on my way over here?"

"What?" she breathed, her eyes closing in bliss.

"Your little owlet's family. Mom and Dad were circling the vineyard, and then one of them flew to the nesting box. When I passed by, I could hear Junior demanding his supper."

She smiled without opening her eyes. "I'm glad he's back where he belongs."

"Just as you belong here, with me."

"But how can we—" She gasped as he snagged the hem of her top and tugged it off to reveal her breasts in the shimmering moonlight.

"There's a way." He bent his head to lick the moisture from her soft flesh. "We just have to find it." His tongue gently laved her, eliciting shudders of delight.

Again, she tried to voice her doubt, but he kissed her before she could speak. This time the earth and water and sky all swirled together, obliterating her fears. The mindless joy of passion beckoned, and she reached for it, returning Max's kiss with sudden abandon. Desire swept through her like a flash fire, and with it came a burning need to get as close to him as possible. She wrapped her legs around his waist and felt the heat of his erection pressing against her lower body as she clung to him.

Max groaned and clasped her hips as they rocked together in mutual hunger. But after only a brief interval, she felt him pushing her away. Uttering a soft sound of protest, she lifted her head to gaze at him in confusion. "Max, what's wrong?"

Breathing a bit harder than normal, he placed his hands on her shoulders and held her at arm's length. "Nothing's wrong, love. I just reached the end of my endurance. One more second of what we were doing and I wouldn't have been able to stop. I don't think that would be wise, considering we don't have any form of birth control available." He gave her a quick hard kiss, then released her and moved back a few inches.

"There is, however, a limit to my fortitude." His eyes narrowed as his gaze lowered to her naked breasts, and he tossed her the tank top which had been hooked on his arm. "You'd better put that on and head for home. The way you look right now is wearing me down fast."

She didn't want to leave, not with so many things left unresolved between them. A reckless inner voice dared her to stay and risk the consequences. But at the same time, his restraint struck a chord deep in her heart. He was trying to prove he was worthy of her trust. Yet the unsated desire that burned brightly in his eyes, told her she'd better leave quickly if she valued the offer. Hastily, she pulled on her top. "We haven't settled anything," she said, stalling.

"I know. But I don't think I can carry on a rational discussion right now. I have to go to Los Angeles tomorrow, but I'll call you in the afternoon, when I get back."

"Max..."

"Good night, love," he said firmly. "We'll work everything out tomorrow."

She headed for home, nascent hope shining in the midst of her uncertainty, as brightly as the moon that lit the dark sky above. But as she climbed over the last pasture fence, a shadow dimmed the moon's light, making her glance up. Leaden storm clouds were moving in with surprising speed, blocking out the light from the moon and stars. As she watched their ominous approach, an inexplicable sense of impending doom began to press down on her.

10

LIANA AWAKENED TO THE tap-tap of raindrops against her bedroom window. According to her bedside clock it was seven in the morning, but the room was still quite dark. She allowed herself one good stretch, then got up and headed for the bathroom. The sun might not be out, but a full day's work lay ahead of her, including a trip to town for supplies. She wanted most of it out of the way before Max called in the afternoon.

"Max," she whispered, staring at her reflection in the bathroom mirror. Just saying his name stirred a glowing warmth inside her that seemed to shine from her eyes. Her affection for John had been strong, but he'd never inspired this kind of soaring elation. Would her father notice the change and question it? Twin worry creases appeared between her dark eyebrows. Explaining her love for Max wouldn't be easy.

For that matter, a lot of major obstacles still lay in her path. Last night, Max had sounded so confident about finding solutions, but the dreary light of morning seemed to resurrect her doubts and magnify them. She'd told him she wanted to stay, but now the repercussions of such a move nagged at her. If her father lost the ranch, it would mean finding employment and a new place to live. Her income from the winery in Oregon would be drastically reduced, because she couldn't in good conscience keep drawing the same amount if she weren't working there anymore.

Then there was the question of Max's intentions. He'd said that he wanted her to stay, that she belonged here with him. But what exactly did that mean? He hadn't mentioned anything like love or a permanent commitment, now that she thought of it. And hadn't Sybille warned that he had a problem in those areas?

Liana rubbed her forehead to ease the tension that was rapidly turning into a headache. Maybe she should just stop thinking about it until she heard what Max had to say. Determined to do just that, she turned on the faucet and splashed cold water on her face. After all, as bad as things looked right now, they probably couldn't get any worse.

WEARY FROM A LONG morning with potential distributors promoting Valentin wines, Max steered his pickup into its parking place beside his house. Because of the heavy rain, he'd started for home earlier than originally planned, and the drive from Los Angeles had been slow and exhausting. But now that he'd arrived safely, the only thing on his mind was arranging to meet Liana and getting things straightened out. First, he'd tell her he loved her—he'd finally decided that last night. He had also devised a possible solution to their problems.

He got out of the truck and started for the back door of the house, but halted abruptly when he saw a hunched figure lurking around the back of the larger

main house. He moved a little closer and recognized Jeff
Moser's distinctively blond hair. Probably spent the
day in bed with Sybille, Max thought in disgust. But he
decided to investigate anyway.

Coming up behind the younger man as he peered in
a window, Max asked, "Looking for someone?"

Jeff started guiltily, and whipped around. "I—uh—I
was wondering where, uh, Sybille might be." His rain-
soaked hair hung in sodden clumps, framing his thin
face, and Max wondered anew about Sybille's current
taste in men.

"I don't know," Max replied. "I've been gone since
this morning. Is anything wrong?"

The pale blue eyes shifted uneasily. "No . . . That is,
I hope—" He swallowed nervously. "I don't think so. I
just needed to talk to her. She hasn't answered the
phone all day, and there doesn't seem to be anybody in
the house."

Again, Max sensed something wasn't quite right. "I
have a key. Why don't we go in and take a look
around?"

Silent gloom reigned inside the house. Max switched
on a few lights as they passed through the immaculate
kitchen and dining room. He called Sybille's name several times as they checked the equally pristine living
room and started upstairs. There was no response. The
door to her bedroom stood ajar, and when he pushed
it completely open a disturbing sight awaited.

Max had never cared for the scarlet-and-black color
theme. It made him think of a bordello. But the room
had always been scrupulously neat, on the few occa-

sions he'd glimpsed it. Now, Sybille's bedroom stood in shocking disarray. The red satin sheets were twisted and half off the bed, clothes were strewn everywhere, and a perfume bottle and several cosmetics jars lay broken with their contents spilled on the black carpet. The ornate cheval glass that stood in the corner had been shattered, and a heavy gold-handled hairbrush lay at its base.

Concern furrowed Max's brow as he quickly scanned the room and the adjoining bathroom. "She's not here," he announced to Jeff who'd hung back. "But someone's really trashed the place. Maybe I should contact the police."

"Wait!" Jeff shoved his hands in the pockets of his jeans, his expression even more distressed. "I—uh—can explain the mess. We sort of had a fight last night."

Max knew all about Sybille's volatile temper. She'd thrown things at his father more than once. But the extent of the damage here surprised him. "A lovers' quarrel?" he asked dryly.

Jeff's gaze dropped to the toes of his running shoes. "Something like that. How did you guess?"

Max nearly laughed. *The kid must think I'm blind and deaf.* "Call it intuition. I've had a little experience with upset women myself. Why don't you tell me what happened?"

An almost-pathetic look of relief touched Jeff's features when he glanced up. "Maybe I should. There isn't anyone else I can talk to. Sybille made me swear not to let on about us, but since you already know..." Nervously he raked a hand through his damp hair. "The whole thing started when I told her I wouldn't be coming around anymore."

Max gave the demolished room a meaningful look. "I take it she didn't receive the news gracefully."

Jeff's expression turned incredulous. "Man, I've never seen her like that before. At first she tried to talk me into staying—you know, coming on to me. When that didn't work, she started throwing things and screaming at me, accusing me of all kinds of crazy stuff. Then she got it into her head that I had a thing for Liana Castillo, 'cause I'd been spending some time working on her dad's truck. I tried to tell her how crazy that was, that there wasn't anyone else, but she wouldn't listen."

"So you weren't leaving her for another woman?" Max prompted.

"Naw." He ducked his head, as if embarrassed. "I just didn't feel right about doin' it with her anymore, you know? I mean, at first it was kind of exciting, having someone like her coming on to me. Heck, I know I'm not in her league. But she acted like I was something special."

He scowled and shrugged. "Lately, though, she's been different. She always wants to know where I've been, and what I've been doing. Every time I went over to the Castillo place, she was all over me with questions."

Irritation made Max grit his teeth, but he suppressed it. "What kind of questions?"

"Oh, everything. She wanted to know what Liana was doing, how the place looked, stuff like that. She even asked about Liana's dad—although I think she was hoping to hear bad news about him."

Max nodded encouragingly. "What made you think that?"

"At first it was just a feeling I had. But last night, when she started in about me having a thing for Liana, she just went kind of nuts and began screaming all kinds of weird things about the Castillos."

A small alarm sounded in Max's mind. She hadn't done it for a long time, but when Sybille lost her temper, the results could be far-reaching. He remembered too well the terrible fights she and his father used to have. "What exactly did she say?" he asked carefully.

Jeff shuffled his feet and looked uncomfortable. "Really crazy stuff. Some of it I didn't even understand. She was raving about how they were responsible for her son's death. Then she started yelling about some land, and how she wouldn't let them take it away from her too. I tried to calm her down, but she just got madder. When she began talking about killing people, I decided it was time to leave."

The alarm sounded louder in Max's mind. He glanced about the room again and a bulge in the draperies caught his eye. When he went to investigate, he discovered a powerful pair of binoculars fastened to a tripod. Peering through them, he got a close-up view of the Castillo ranch buildings. For some reason, the sight filled him with dread. "She said she was going to kill Liana and her father?"

"Something like that. She kept talking about poisoned wine and accidents. But like I said, she didn't make much sense. Say, where are you going?"

Max didn't pause on his way to the stairs. "To call Liana." He couldn't believe that Sybille would actually follow through on her threats, but he wasn't taking any chances. He dialed the Castillos' number from the kitchen phone, but all he heard was endless ringing.

There's probably a very simple explanation, he told himself, slamming the receiver down and heading for the door.

Jeff followed, looking anxious. "You don't think she'd really—"

Max turned around on the porch and cut him off abruptly. "No. But I don't want her bothering the Castillos, either. I think I'll just run over there and make sure everything's all right. You don't have to hang around if you don't want to. I'll handle Sybille when she returns."

Looking immensely relieved, Jeff nodded and sprinted through the driving rain toward the ancient truck he'd left parked at the side of the house.

As Max started his own truck, however, his sense of impending trouble increased. The truck fishtailed as he accelerated down the drive.

LIANA PARKED HER father's truck in front of the back door, and got out to unload the groceries she'd purchased that morning. On her first trip into the house she set her purse and two full bags on the kitchen counter, and called out a greeting to her father. When he didn't answer, she went looking for him, thinking he'd probably dozed off, but pinpricks of anxiety began to torment her as she checked one room after another and found no sign of him.

Where can he be? she wondered, trying not to panic. Granted, he'd become pretty skilled with the crutches, but surely he wouldn't go out in the rain? Her worry increased when she remembered his reaction that morning when the last bank called and turned down their loan application. He'd looked as if someone had sucked the life out of him. Shortly afterward, he'd retreated to his room and hadn't come out even when she announced she was leaving for town.

Considering his earlier dejection, his absence now raised disturbing thoughts. Maybe he'd gone to the stable for some reason—although she couldn't think how he would have managed it with a cast and crutches in the rain and mud. She dashed outside, pulling up the hood of her jacket against the unrelenting downpour, but when she reached the stable's dim interior, only the soft whickering of horses answered her call. She closed her eyes in silent prayer against the sudden fear that gripped her. He wouldn't do anything rash, would he? Her heart began to hammer in her chest as she searched the other outbuildings. There wasn't a sign of him anywhere.

The sound of a car approaching drew her attention as she ran back to the house. A compact car pulled up next to the truck and a familiar figure got out.

Dressed in a yellow rain slicker, Sybille approached with a wild look in her eyes. "Liana, you must come quickly. There's been an accident. Your father's hurt!"

The beating of her heart escalated to a painful level. "What happened? Where is he?"

Sybille clutched at Liana's arm, pulling her toward the truck. "I don't know how it happened, but he's lying in an irrigation ditch, and I couldn't get him out myself. I called for an emergency crew, but who knows how long they'll take to get here. Follow me in the truck, and I'll show you where he is. Maybe we can do something."

Liana didn't need further prodding. She raced into the house and grabbed her keys, knocking her purse and one of the grocery bags to the floor. Ignoring the mess, she ran back outside, jumped into the truck and started it.

To her surprise, Sybille drove off toward the dirt road that bisected their properties. As Liana followed, her anxiety grew. What in the world had her father been doing out here? For that matter, how had he gone so far without a car? They followed the hilly dirt road until it turned to gravel on an adjoining piece of land. The rain pelted against the windshield so hard, the old wipers barely kept it clear, and Liana nearly ran into Sybille's car when she stopped unexpectedly.

They were in a fairly deserted section of the valley, with not a residence in sight. The gravel road continued north to the mountains; to the right of the road lay a large citrus orchard bordered by an old irrigation ditch complete with an ancient wooden sluice gate.

Sybille got out of her car and started toward the ditch, motioning for Liana to follow. She complied, dreading what she'd find.

Her father lay at the bottom of the six-foot-deep channel with at least five inches of water lapping at his cast and uninjured leg. His upper body was propped against the slanted dirt wall of the ditch, but that afforded no protection from the pouring rain. The storm had caused a tremendous backup of water behind the gate, and it creaked ominously as she surveyed the situation.

"Dad, can you hear me? Are you all right?" she called anxiously. He looked up and gestured feebly with one hand. His lips moved and she strained forward, trying to hear. Suddenly an excruciating pain exploded at the back of her head. Everything went black as the earth gave way beneath her feet.

MAX BROUGHT HIS TRUCK to a skidding halt in front of the Castillo house and got out at a run. When no one answered at the front, he tried the kitchen door. It swung open at his touch, and his misgivings grew when he saw the spilled groceries and Liana's purse lying on the floor. He stepped inside, calling her name, but the house seemed to reverberate with ominous silence.

After a fruitless check of the ranch's other buildings, he went back to his truck to consider his next move. That was when he saw the tire tracks heading toward the dirt road that served as a boundary between his vineyards and the Castillos' ranch—the same road he and Liana had raced down on horseback not so long ago.

He studied the tire-tread impressions carefully and decided they had to belong to Frank's old truck, although the imprint was blurred in places by the marks of other tires that had preceded them. Hard to tell how long they'd been there, but they looked fairly fresh. The question was, why would Liana or her father go driving on that road in a rainstorm? All of the horses had been in the barn when he checked. There wasn't much of interest in the segment of the valley where those tracks led. But a gut feeling compelled him to get in his truck and follow them.

When he reached the point where the dirt road turned to gravel, he stopped to reconsider. There hadn't been any sign of the Castillo truck. Maybe he was on a wild-goose chase. The tire tracks appeared to continue onto the rocky surface, but he knew there was a fork in the road just past the next two rises. How would he choose the right direction to follow? "If there is a right direction," he muttered to himself, his conviction faltering. Maybe he should go back to the ranch and see if Liana had returned. Frowning, he pondered the options a moment longer, then made his decision and put the truck in gear.

LIANA STRUGGLED OUT of the painful darkness that held her captive, to the reality of cold wet misery. Her entire body ached, but the most intense pain was at the back of her head. Vaguely she heard her father's voice calling her name. She shook her head and heard it again, louder this time. Forcing her eyes open, she discovered she was lying on her stomach in muddy water.

She raised her head, from where it had been cushioned on her arm, and looked around in confusion until she saw her father sprawled a few feet away. Suddenly, everything shifted into sharp focus. She was in the irrigation ditch. The last thing she remembered she'd been looking down into it; now she was lying at the bottom. To make matters worse, the rain had continued to fall relentlessly.

"Liana, are you hurt?" His voice sounded weak and strained, as if he were in terrible pain.

Forgetting her own discomfort, she hauled herself up on hands and knees and crawled over to him. "Don't worry about me. What about you? How did you get down here?"

His expression hardened. "Same way you did." He nodded toward a point beyond her shoulder, "But she didn't conk me over the head before she pushed me in. She lured me out here with a big lie about you falling into this ditch. I was so scared at the thought of you being hurt, I believed her." He gripped Liana's arm and she saw the panic in his eyes. "She's gone crazy, honey. She wants to kill us."

Frantic, Liana twisted around and saw Sybille standing on top of the sluice gate. She was bent over and yanking on the handwheel that raised the lower half of the gate. In a horrifying flash, Liana realized Sybille was trying to open it. If she succeeded, the ditch would be flooded almost instantly. "Why are you doing this?" Liana cried out.

Sybille turned around, an ugly look on her face. "Because I refuse to let you Castillos ruin my life again," she sneered. "That little slut sister of yours did when she killed my son. Now you're trying to do it, by stealing Valentin land."

In spite of her precarious position, incredulous fury drove Liana to her feet. Although her life was in danger, she refused to let the woman continue with her old self-delusions. "What are you talking about? Serena didn't kill anyone. It was your son who was driving the car that night, remember? If anyone was a killer, *he* was. As for the land, we were only trying to keep what was ours."

"It won't be yours when you're dead." Sybille bent to tug on the wheel again and was rewarded with a rusty squeak. The gate itself groaned and creaked louder.

Galvanized into action by the sound, Liana began scrambling up the side of the muddy embankment. She had to stop Sybille before she got that gate open. If the water behind it was released, her father would drown.

Sybille's voice rang out: "If you don't stop, I'll shoot you!"

Liana looked up and saw the heavy pistol in the woman's hand. Reluctantly she let go of the thick root she'd been using to haul herself up. "You'll never get away with this," she said, desperately trying to reason with her.

Smirking, Sybille went back to wrestling with the recalcitrant wheel with one hand, while keeping the gun trained on Liana and her father with the other. "Why not? I managed all the other times."

Alarmed, Liana asked, "What other times?"

"The honey wine, for one. Did you know that it was poisoned? That was one of my more clever plans. Imagine my disappointment when it didn't turn out to be lethal."

Dear heaven, the woman really is mad! Liana thought, wiping the rain out of her eyes. She went to crouch protectively beside her father, but she knew she had to keep Sybille talking. Whenever the woman spoke, her efforts to move the wheel slowed a little. "How did you poison the wine? I had it analyzed and they couldn't tell."

"Sumac," Sybille announced with pride. "Or if you prefer, poison oak. I read about it in a book once. You just plant it near the beehive and the bees poison the honey by gathering the pollen. Clever, no? Then there were all of the little accidents I arranged for your father. Unfortunately, none of them worked too well, either—except the one with the horse."

Almost afraid of what she'd hear, Liana asked anyway. "Are you talking about the afternoon my father was injured?"

"I told you," he interjected weakly. "How did you do it, Sybille? Was it a gun, like I suspected?"

"A pellet gun." Grunting a little with the effort of her ongoing attempts to turn the wheel, she managed a laugh. "I was especially proud of that one, because I even remembered to pick up the used pellets while you were at the hospital. No evidence, you see? And that black horse hates me so much, it was a simple matter to shoo him into the stall the day you were cleaning it,"

she added to Liana. "But this is the best plan of all. I'll
get rid of both of you at once and it will look like an accident." The weathered boards of the sluice gate made
a sharp sound, as if in protest, and water shot out from
several cracks in the structure.

A combination of fear and helpless rage swept over
Liana. She couldn't allow Sybille to get away with this.
Maybe she should risk the accuracy of Sybille's aim and
make a rush for the top of the ditch. . . .

The sound of an approaching vehicle caught her attention.

Sybille must have heard it, too, because she glanced
up and shouted a furious, "No!" Her efforts at the
handwheel became frantic.

Liana uttered a silent prayer as the hum of the engine
grew louder then abruptly ceased. She heard the slamming of a door and the thud of running feet. Max's
voice rang out. "Sybille, for God's sake, what are you
doing?" Then he appeared at the edge of the ditch. His
face registered shock and concern when he saw Liana
and her father. But when his eyes swept to the leaking
sluice gate and Sybille, his expression turned thunder-
ous. "Let go of that wheel and get off of there—now!"
The sheer authority of his voice made Liana's heart leap
with hope.

But Sybille just shook her head and yanked harder,
causing another raspy squeak. "You don't understand,
Max. I'm doing this for you, too. You'd be able to see
that, if you weren't beguiled by her." She paused,
panting, and jerked her head toward Liana. "But then,

I shouldn't be surprised—not after the way her sister trapped my poor Rennie. If he'd—"

Max's crude expletive cut her off. "Come off it, Sybille. I know as well as anyone what a user Rennie was. If anyone was trapped it must have been Serena. Now, stop acting crazy and come down here before I have to come and get you."

A belligerent look crossed Sybille's face. "You can't stop me. I've waited too long for this."

When he started toward the sluice gate, Sybille brought the gun into view just as Liana cried out a warning, "Max, don't! She has a gun!"

Eyes narrowed with evil intent, Sybille brandished the weapon. "Stay back, or I'll kill you too. I swear it."

Max didn't even slow his stride. "I'm not going to let you harm Liana or her father."

"I said, stop!"

Sybille stamped her foot and the wooden structure beneath her made a terrible cracking noise. Several of the slow leaks began to gush water. When Max still didn't comply, she raised the pistol, and took aim.

Liana screamed, "Max, no!" But it was too late. The gun went off, and Max staggered back clutching his left shoulder. At the same time, Sybille uttered a hoarse shriek and seemed to wobble, her arms flailing. The pistol flew through the air and landed in the ditch just as Sybille lost her balance completely and fell over the far side of the gate. Dimly, Liana heard a thud and a splash. But all her concern was focused on Max. He hadn't fallen, but his shoulder was bleeding, staining the tan fabric of his trench coat. He stumbled a little as he came back to the edge of the ditch.

"Max!" she cried. "Oh, dear God, are you all right?"

He shook his head, as if to clear it. The sluice gate groaned again, and he gave it a sharp glance. "Don't worry about me, right now. We have to get you and your father out of there before that gate lets go." He scanned the area, then shrugged out of his overcoat and suit jacket, wincing a little. "I don't have a rope, so these will have to do." She watched anxiously as he tied the two garments together, then stripped off his slacks and added them to the makeshift rope.

A large fissure appeared near the bottom of the wooden gate and water came rushing through. "We've got to hurry," Max shouted as he slid down the six-foot embankment and rushed over to where her father lay. The water level had risen to midcalf, which meant that her father's legs were completely submerged.

"This isn't going to be easy," Max muttered, "but we'll manage. Liana, help me get him over to the side."

"What about your shoulder?" she cried.

"It's not that bad. Come on, we have to hurry." He crouched down in front of her father. "Frank, I'm going to prop you up against the side of the ditch, preferably standing up. Then we'll loop the rope under your arms, and I'll pull you up from above while Liana pushes from down here."

Her father wagged his head in protest. "You don't owe me that, Valentin. You don't owe me anything. Just get Liana out before it's too late."

Max shook his head, seemingly oblivious to the pelting rain and the widening red stain on the shoulder of his shirt. "Look, Frank, this isn't the time for any of your stubborn pride. I love your daughter at least as much as you do, and her happiness is of primary importance to me. If anything happened to you, it would hurt her, so like it or not, I'm going to save you. Now, do you think you could give me a little help in doing that?"

He loves me. In spite of their circumstances, the thought caused a shock wave in Liana's consciousness, but she didn't have time to dwell on it.

An odd light gleamed in her father's eyes as he stared back at Max, but after a moment he nodded his head. "I got banged up when I fell, but I think I can still stand on my good leg."

Between the three of them they got him upright and half lying against the side of the ditch. Using the roots that protruded from the muddy incline, Max hauled himself up. Liana heard him grunt in pain, but he didn't slow down.

Using the improvised rope, they began the arduous process of dragging her father out of the ditch. As they worked, the noise from the sluice gate increased to a roar. The water level rose to Liana's knees. She pushed with all her might, but the going was slow because of the cast's added weight. Her muscles felt strained to the breaking point, but just when she thought she couldn't take another moment, Max gave a mighty heave and pulled her father over the edge.

At that moment, she heard an explosive crack behind her and, without a glance back, she grasped for a nearby root. A massive rush of water caught her legs, dragging her sideways. Screaming, she grabbed the root with her other hand and frantically held on. Just as her hands began to slip, Max leaned over the edge, his arms outstretched.

"Grab my hands, love," he called urgently.

For a panic-stricken moment she didn't think she could do it. Taking his hands would mean letting go of the root and running the risk of being swept away by the rushing water. What if his grip wasn't strong enough? What if his hands slipped?

"Trust me, Liana." The words were half command, half plea, and when she looked into his eyes, her doubts vanished. She let go with one hand and he caught it in his. But then her other hand slipped from the root and for one horrifying moment, man and water played a desperate game of tug-of-war. She cried out in fear. But with one forceful tug, Max hauled her up over the edge. She felt his powerful arms close around her, and as they lay on the wet ground, gasping and hugging, his frantic murmur filled her ear. "Liana, I love you, I love you."

"I know. I love you, too." She clung to him, her tears of relief mixing with the rain. "When Sybille shot you, I nearly died."

He tensed. "Damn, I forgot about Sybille. Did you see what happened to her after she shot me?"

Closing her eyes at the awful memory of the gun's explosion, Liana shook her head. "She lost her balance and fell into the water on the far side of the gate. That's the last I saw of her." Her eyes opened wide in horror. "Max, when the gate broke, she must have been—"

Max shoved himself to his feet. "I'll go look. You check on your father."

"Wait!" She delayed him with a hand on his arm. "Shouldn't we do something about your shoulder? It's still bleeding."

"I think it's just a flesh wound." He gave her a quick kiss, then headed for the broken sluice gate.

Switching her concern to her father, she stepped over to where he lay. His face was gray with pain and exposure, but he was fully conscious. "Liana, thank heaven he got you out. I heard the gate give way and I was afraid—"

"Shh! Don't upset yourself about it now. I'm safe." She removed her jacket and held it over his head to protect him from the rain. "What about you? Do you have any idea how badly you're hurt?"

"It's not as bad as it could have been. I ache all over, but my arms and good leg still work."

"Hang on, then. Max went to look for Sybille, but as soon as he comes back we'll get you to a hospital."

He clutched her arm with sudden urgency. "None of this would've happened if I hadn't been so stubborn about hanging on to the ranch. No piece of land is worth dying for and if it hadn't been for Max we would be dead. I'll owe him for the rest of my life. But I'm still not sure I like the guy." He shook his head. "He told me he loves you—I don't know how I feel about that."

She took a fortifying breath and said, "Well, you might as well get used to the idea because I love *him*, Dad. I'm sorry if that makes you unhappy, but I can't change how I feel."

The grooves in her father's wrinkled forehead deepened. "Liana, are you sure . . ." His words trailed off at the sound of Max's approaching footsteps.

"I found her." The dark note in Max's voice told them the news wasn't good. "She must've gone with the gate when it broke. Some of the lumber got jammed about a hundred yards from here. . . ." He sighed heavily. "Her body's stuck there under the water. I'll need a crew to get her out, so that'll have to wait for a while."

Her father grunted softly. "Kind of poetic justice—her getting killed by the means she intended for us." He turned to address Max. "Thank God you found us in time."

Max grimaced. "I almost didn't." He gave her father a tired smile. "Looks like you're going to get another ride in the back of my truck. Unless you think you should wait for an ambulance."

The two men exchanged a long look, and then her father nodded. "I guess you'll do." Something in the way he said it made Liana wonder if more than one question had been answered.

As LIANA SLOWLY WALKED through the vineyard's neat rows, lambent moonlight painted the grape leaves a silvery green. Only a week had passed since Sybille's violent end and yet in ways it seemed longer. Sometimes specters of that horrible day swooped down to haunt her, but the images lost power with each passing day. Thank heaven, Max's wound had proved to be superficial, and hadn't given him too much discomfort.

Not that she'd seen him as much as she would have liked. He'd been terribly busy dealing with the police investigation and a myriad of other complications brought on by Sybille's death. He came by every evening to have supper with her and her father, and the two men seemed to be forging a tentative friendship. Unfortunately, she and Max didn't really have any time alone. Aside from the spectacular good-night kisses they'd shared on the back porch, along with some fervently whispered words of love, nothing had been settled between them.

When he'd called earlier and asked her to meet him in the vineyard that evening, her heart had skipped in anticipation. Maybe tonight they would be able to talk about the future.

The gauzy pink material of her sundress floated softly against her body in the balmy night air. When she inhaled, the sweet reassuring scent of rich soil and lush greenery filled her senses. Max was right, this was where she belonged. Closing her eyes, she whirled around, letting the joy of that thought sink in. She nearly fell over when Max's voice broke the stillness of the air.

"First a mermaid in a pond, now a fairy princess dancing in my vineyard. Your talents seem to be endless, my love."

"Max!" She ran to him and felt the glory of his arms closing around her once more. He picked her up and swung her around and for the first time in days she heard his deep laughter ring out.

Remembering his injury, she tried to wriggle free. "You'll hurt your shoulder."

He merely laughed again and held her tighter. "Nothing hurts when I'm holding you, love." So she wrapped her arms around his neck and kissed him with abandon, until he finally allowed her feet to touch the ground again.

"Mmm, will you promise to greet me every night like that?" He nuzzled her neck and nipped playfully at her earlobe.

"How can I promise that when I don't know if I'll see you every night?" She ducked her head, forestalling his efforts to kiss her again.

"You would if you married me."

She gaped at him. "Are you serious?"

"So serious, I even asked your father for his approval."

Astonished, she laughed. "How incredibly old-fashioned."

"I know. But I also knew you'd be happier if he went along with the idea—which he did. Ever since you came back to the valley, I've been thinking about all kinds of old-fashioned things—like love and commitment and families." He touched his mouth to hers with seductive tenderness. "And waking up with you beside me every morning. That one has special appeal."

She wanted to say yes, but it wasn't quite that simple. For one thing, her father's future had to be decided. "Max, I can't agree to marry you until I get a few things straightened out in my life."

"If you're talking about your father, I have a proposal. Ever since we went riding, I've been thinking I'd like to have a horse or two around. Since Sonny and I seem to get along, I thought I would offer to buy him. We could leave the stable where it is for the time being and keep one big pasture for the horses while the rest of the land is converted to vineyards. If your father accepts my offer, he could move into my grandparents' house."

She gazed at him in amazement. "If he takes over your place, will you move to the big house?"

"Uh-huh. It's been legally mine ever since my father died. I just let Sybille use it because she'd taken it over so completely when she first moved in. I'm changing that, though. The whole place is being overhauled. Not one trace of her will be left when it's finished."

Again, her heart told her to say yes, but there was one aspect that hadn't been defined to her satisfaction. "All of that sounds great, but where do I fit in your grand scheme?"

He stroked her cheek gently. "As my partner, my wife, my love." He grinned and winked. "And as my accountant, if you want the job. We could do great things together."

She knew without reservation that she wanted all of the above, but before she could tell him, a shadow crossed over them, drawing their attention to the sky. A small barn owl soared overhead, his wingbeats silent and graceful.

"Max, is that—?"

"Yeah. His parents taught him to fly a few days ago. I've been meaning to tell you, but I've been so busy, I kept forgetting." He turned her head until their gazes met. "I'd better warn you, if you take me up on the other job offers, I may add another."

Teasing him with a wide-eyed look, she asked, "Do you want me to raise orphan owls?"

"No." He pulled her close and gave her a long, sultry kiss. "But I would like to see a couple of little Bambi-eyed Valentins running around. Would you be interested in helping me with that?"

Children? Good Lord, he *was* serious. "I might need a little convincing on the idea. I've never pictured myself as the mothering type."

He chuckled softly and began to caress her back with finesse. "I can be very good at convincing."

She moaned as sensual delight coursed through her body. "I know. I think you had me beguiled from the start."

Tilting her head up for his kiss, he paused just before their lips met. "No more than you bewitched me with those Bambi eyes. Did I hear a 'Yes, Max, I'll marry you' in there somewhere?"

The answer came bubbling out of her like sparkling champagne. "Yes, Max. Yes! Yes! Yes!" Then her words were consumed by his intoxicating kiss.

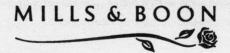

This month's
irresistible novels from
TEMPTATION

THE BAD BOY by Roseanne Williams

Meet Brew Brodrick—another in Temptation's sinfully sexy
line-up of men under the banner Rebels & Rogues. Rebel.
Tough. Street-wise. Brew had a past and a difficult attitude to
match. Social blue blood. Gorgeous. Cautious. Meri
Whitworth had one too many secrets. Brew represented a
threat she didn't want to face...

BEGUILED by Dawn Carroll

Liana Castillo had sworn never to return to her home town.
She couldn't face the painful memories of a horrifying night of
violence. For fourteen years she had kept her vow—until Max
Valentin threatened to put her father out of business.

DEVIL TO PAY by Renee Roszel

Alyssa had responsibilities and what she didn't need was to fall
for embittered Rourk Rountree. He was devilishly sexy, but
he would send her world completely out of control...

BORROWED TIME by Regan Forest

Flashes of Tombstone in 1882 crowded in on Sarah
Christianson—the image of the Bird Cage Theater, the
frightened face of Josie, a young prostitute, and the presence
of the man Sarah had left behind...but had never stopped
loving.

Spoil yourself next month
with these four novels from

TEMPTATION

THE MAVERICK by Janice Kaiser

Meet Alex Townsend—another in Temptation's sinfully sexy
line-up of men under the banner Rebels & Rogues. Rogue
reporter. Loner. His motto: live dangerously. Gabriella Lind.
Gorgeous. Sexy. She played it safe…until she met Alex.

MICHAEL'S WIFE by Tracy Morgan

Sloan Lassiter had listened to Michael Varner's stories about
his wife, Jesse, so often during the months they had been held
hostage that he felt he knew her…intimately. Michael had
sadly died in captivity, but now Sloan was free and he knew he
had to meet Michael's wife…

THE SUNDOWNER by Madeline Harper

When Kara Selwyn inherited half of the Sundowner, a shabby
watering hole on the Gulf of Florida, she planned to sell
it—fast. Until her new partner, rough-hewn Nick Fleming, put
his foot down. Could she charm him into giving her what she
wanted?

TRYING PATIENCE by Carla Neggers

Chic women in lacy lingerie were Jake Farr's preference, so he
wasn't amused when he was set up with Patience Madrid—
very much a natural woman. Persuaded into temporarily
sharing an apartment together, who would be trying whose
patience?

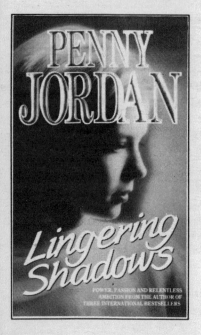